—— Robert Louis
Stevenson

KIDNAPPED

Published in this edition 1997 by Peter Haddock Ltd,
Pinfold Lane, Bridlington, East Yorkshire YO16 5BT

© 1997 this arrangement, text and illustrations,
Geddes & Grosset Ltd, David Dale House,
New Lanark, Scotland

© original text John Kennett

Illustrated by John Marshall

ISBN 0 7105 1018 7

Printed and bound in France
by Maury Eurolivres

10 9 8 7 6 5 4 3 2 1

Contents

To the Reader

When you have seen and enjoyed a film or TV programme that has been made from some famous book, you may decide to read the book.

Then what happens? You get the book and, it's more than likely, you get a shock as well! You turn ten or twenty pages, and nothing seems to *happen*. Where are all the lively people and exciting incidents? When, you say, will the author get down to telling the story? In the end you will probably throw the book aside and give it up. Now, why is that?

Well, perhaps the author was writing for adults and not for children. Perhaps the book was written a long time ago, when people had more time for reading and liked nothing better than a book that would keep them entertained for weeks.

We think differently today. That's why some of these wonderful books have been retold for you. If you enjoy them in this shorter form, then when you are older you will go back to the original books, and enjoy all the more the stories they have to tell.

About the Author

Robert Louis Stevenson, novelist, essayist and poet, was born in Edinburgh in 1850 into a famous family of lighthouse engineers. Although he never enjoyed good health, he travelled widely, finally making his home in the tropical island of Samoa, where he died in 1894. The Samoan name for him was Tusitala, "storyteller".

Stevenson's poems for children are collected in *A Child's Garden of Verses*. Among his many tales of adventure, *Catriona* is of special interest to readers of *Kidnapped*, since in it he tells of further adventures of David Balfour.

CHAPTER ONE
The House of Shaws

It was on a morning early in the month of June 1751 that I took the key for the last time out of the door of my father's house. I did not once look back. The sun was shining on the hilltops as I walked through the village.

Mr Campbell, the minister of Essendean, was waiting for me by his garden gate. His face creased in a smile. "Well, Davie, lad," he said, "have you had breakfast? Good! I'll walk to the ford, to see you on your way."

We walked on in silence.

"Are ye sorry to leave Essendean?" he asked.

"Well, sir," I answered, "I've been very happy here – but then I've never been anywhere else. Now that my parents are dead, I want to see something of the world."

"There's something I must tell you," he said. "When your mother died and your father knew that he was sickening for his end, he gave me a letter, which he said was your inheritance. 'When my house is sold,' he said, 'start him off to the house of Shaws, near Cramond. That's where I came from, and it's where Davie should return.'"

"The house of Shaws?" I cried. "What had my father to do with the house of Shaws?"

"I don't know," said the minister, "but the name of that family is the name you bear – Balfour of Shaws. It's an old and famous name, Davie, and though your father came here as a schoolmaster it was clear to us all that he was a gentleman of good family and had known better times. Now, lad, here's the letter he gave me."

He handed me the letter, which was addressed in these words: "To Ebenezer Balfour, Esquire, of the house of Shaws, to be delivered by my son, David Balfour."

"Mr Campbell," I stammered, "would you go, if you were in my shoes?"

"Aye," he answered, "that I would. A big lad like you ought to get to Cramond, which is near Edinburgh, in two days of walking."

I walked on, my head in a whirl, until we came to the ford. Here, Mr Campbell bid me goodbye.

I shouldered my bundle, set out over the ford and up the hill on the farther side. When I came to the top, I took my last look at Essendean and the big trees in the churchyard where my father and mother lay; then, squaring my shoulders, I went down the other side.

I stood, two days later, on top of a hill, from which all the country fell away before me down to the sea. In the middle of this slope, on a long ridge, I saw the smoking chimneys of Edinburgh.

I followed a road that skirted the city to the west, and got a shepherd to point me the way to Cramond.

A little farther on, I began to ask for the house of Shaws. It was a name that surprised everyone I met. People just gaped at it and some seemed almost frightened by it.

I had to find out more about the place. I saw a small cart bumping along a lane, the driver perched on its shaft. I waved him to stop and asked him if he'd heard of it.

He looked at me oddly, like the others. "Aye," he said.

"Is it a great house?" I asked.

"Aye," he said, with narrowed eyes, "it's big enough."

"And what about the folk who live there?"

"Folk?" he cried. "There's no folk there to call folk."

"What?" I said. "Not Mr Ebenezer?"

"Oh, ay," said the man, "there's the laird, to be sure, if it's *him* you're wanting. What's your business there?"

"I thought I might get a job there," I answered.

"What!" cried the carter, so sharply that his horse started; and then, "Well, my lad," he added, "if ye'll take a word from me, ye'll keep clear of the Shaws!"

He drove on, leaving me filled with strange fears. I was tempted, then and there, to turn back. But I'd come so far already that I was bound to go on.

It was nearly sundown when I met a dark, sour-looking woman trudging down a hill. I asked my usual question. She scowled at me, turned sharp about and walked with me back to the summit. She pointed a long finger at a great bulk of building standing on a green in the valley. The house seemed to be a kind of ruin.

"That's the house of Shaws!" the woman cried fiercely. "Blood built it; blood stopped the building of it; blood shall bring it down. I spit upon the ground and crack my thumb at it! Black be its fall! If ye see the laird, tell him this makes the twelve hundred and nineteenth time that Jennet Clouston has cursed him."

It was weird and frightening. Her voice had risen to a shriek. She turned as I stood gaping and was gone. My hair stood on end. To have met a witch, and heard her curses, took all the strength out of my legs.

I sat down and stared at the house of Shaws. It seemed, from there, like the one wing of a great house that had never been finished. What should have been the inner end stood open on the upper floors and showed against the sky with steps and stairs of unfinished masonry.

I sat there until the sun went down, and then, right up against the yellow sky, I saw a wisp of smoke go mounting. At least, I thought, it meant a fire, and warmth.

I rose and went forward by a faint track in the grass. It brought me to stone uprights, with an unroofed lodge beside them and coats of arms upon the top. Instead of iron gates, a pair of hurdles were tied across with a rope.

The nearer I got to the house, the drearier it seemed. Night had begun to fall. In three of the lower windows, which were very narrow and well barred, the changing light of a little fire began to glimmer.

I went forward quietly. When I got close to the house, I

heard a rattle of dishes and someone gave a little, dry cough. There was no other sound, and no dog barked.

The door was a great piece of wood, all studded with nails. I lifted my hand and knocked once. Then I stood and waited. The house had fallen into a dead silence. A whole minute passed and nothing stirred but bats overhead. I knocked again, and listened, but whoever was in that house kept deadly still and must have held his breath.

I was in two minds whether to run away, but anger got the upper hand and I began instead to rain kicks on the door, and to shout out aloud for Mr Balfour.

A moment later and I heard a cough right above me. I jumped back, looked up, and saw a man's head in a tall nightcap and the bell mouth of a blunderbuss at one of the first storey windows.

"The gun's loaded," said a dry, cracked voice.

"I've come here with a letter," I said, "to Mr Ebenezer Balfour of Shaws. Is he here?"

"Put it on the doorstep," was the reply, "and be off."

"I'll do no such thing," I cried. "I'll give it to Mr Balfour himself. It's a letter of introduction."

"Who are ye, yourself?" was the next question.

"They call me David Balfour," I answered.

Even in that dim light I saw the man start. "Is your father dead?" he asked. "Ay, he'll be dead, no doubt. And that's what brings ye knocking at my door. Well, man, I'll let ye in," and he disappeared from the window.

CHAPTER TWO
I Run a Great Danger

I waited. Presently there came a loud rattling of chains and bolts. The door opened a little and shut again behind me as soon as I had slipped inside.

"Go into the kitchen," said the voice.

I groped my way into the kitchen while the bolts crashed home behind me. The fire had burned up fairly bright and showed me the barest room I ever set eyes on. Half a dozen dishes stood on the shelves; the table was laid for supper with a bowl of porridge, a horn spoon and a cup of small beer. There was not another thing in that great stone room but lockfast chests arranged along the wall and in a corner.

The man followed me into the kitchen. He was a mean, stooping, narrow-shouldered, clay-faced creature. His age might have been anything between fifty and seventy. His nightcap was of flannel, and so was the nightgown that he wore over his ragged shirt. He was unshaved; but what distressed me most was that he would neither take his eyes away from me nor look me fairly in the face.

"Are ye hungry?" he asked, glancing at about the level of my knee. "Can you eat that drop of porridge?"

I said I feared it was his own supper.

"Ye may have it," he said, "though I'll take the ale." He drank the cup about half out, then suddenly held out his hand. "Let's see the letter." he said.

"The letter's for Mr Balfour," I answered, "not for you."

"And who do ye think I am?" he asked. "Give me Alexander's letter!"

"You know my father's name?"

"It would be strange if I didn't," he replied, "since he was my own brother. I'm your born uncle, Davie, my man, and you my born nephew. So give us the letter, and sit down and fill your stomach."

I could find no words, but handed him the letter and sat down to eat his stodgy porridge.

He stooped by the fire, turning the letter over and over.

"D'ye know what's in it?" he asked suddenly.

"Sir, you can see for yourself," I said coldly, "that the seal has not been broken."

"Ay," he said, "but what brought ye here?"

"To give the letter," I answered.

"No," he said cunningly, "there's more to it than that. Ye'll be wanting something from me."

"Well," I said, "I did think when I was told that I had well-to-do kinsfolk that they might help me. But I'm no beggar. I've friends of my own that will help me."

"Hoot-toot," said Uncle Ebenezer, "don't fly up at me. We'll agree fine yet."

He took a pull at the beer. "If ye're dry," he said, putting down the cup, "ye'll find water behind the door."

I looked at him with an angry heart. He went on throwing little darting glances at my shoes and stockings. Only once did our eyes met. His gaze shifted away at once.

"How long's your father been dead?" he asked.

"Three weeks, sir."

"He was a secret man," he mused. "He never said much when he was young. Did he ever speak of me?"

"I never knew, till you told me, that he had a brother."

"To think of that!" he said, then came across the room behind me, and hit me a smack upon the shoulder. "We'll agree fine yet!" he cried. "I'm glad I let you in. And now come awa' to your bed."

To my surprise, he lit no lamp or candle, but went out into the dark passage. I followed him, and we groped our way up a flight of steps. He unlocked a door. "This is your room," he said. "Go in, Davie."

I begged a light. "Hoot-toot," said Uncle Ebenezer, "there's a fine moon. I don't agree with lights in a house. I'm afraid of fires. Good night to ye, Davie."

He pulled the door to, and I heard him lock me in.

The room was as cold as a well, and the bed, when I'd found my it, almost as damp. I rolled myself in my plaid, lay down upon the floor under the big bedstead and fell speedily asleep.

With the first peep of day I opened my eyes. I was in a

big room, with fine furniture and lit by three windows. Ten years ago it might have been a pleasant room, but damp and dirt, mice and spiders had done their worst. Many of the windowpanes were broken.

I knocked and shouted until my uncle came and let me out. He led me to the back of the house, where there was a draw-well, and told me to wash my face there.

I went back to the kitchen, where he had lit the fire and was making the porridge. The table was laid with two bowls and two spoons but only one cup of beer.

When we had eaten, my uncle sat in the sun at one of the windows and fired questions at me about Essendean.

At last, he said: "Davie, my man, ye came to the right place when ye came to your Uncle Ebenezer. But while I'm thinking what's the best thing to do with you, you must write no letters and speak no kind of word to anybody; or else – there's my door!"

"If you show me your door again," I said, "I'll take you at your word. I'll not stay where I'm not wanted."

"Hoot-toot," he said, "wait a day or two, Davie – and say nothing to nobody – and as sure as sure, I'll do the right thing by you. There's nobody but you and me left of the name of Balfour."

He rambled on then, about the family and its great days in the past, and how his father began to enlarge the house, and how he had stopped the building as a waste. This put it in my head to give him Jennet Clouston's message.

"The old witch!" he cried. "Curse me, will she? I'll have her roasted on red coals. I'll off and see the magistrate."

He opened a chest, muttering to himself, and got out a very old blue coat and waistcoat and a beaver hat, and taking a stick from the cupboard, was about to leave the house when a thought stopped him dead. "I can't leave you by yourself in the house," he said. "I'll have to lock you out."

The blood rushed to my face. "If you lock me out," I said, "it'll be the last you'll ever see of me."

He turned very pale and sucked his mouth in. "This is no way to talk," he said. "Well, well, I'll not go. That's the end of it."

"Uncle Ebenezer," I said, "you are treating me like a thief. You hate to have me in this house, and you let me see it every minute. Why do you try to keep me, then?"

"I like you fine," he cried, "I can't let you go. Stay here quiet, there's a good lad. Ye'll find that we agree."

"Well, sir," I said, "I'll stay a while. And if we don't agree, I'll do my best to see that it's no fault of mine."

The rest of the day passed fairly well. We had the porridge cold again at noon, and hot porridge at night. My uncle spoke but little, and let me go into a room next door to the kitchen, where I found a large number of books in which I took great pleasure all the afternoon.

And then I found something which worried me a lot. It was an entry on the fly-leaf of one book, in my father's

'To my brother
Ebeneezer
on his fifth
birthday'

handwriting, which said: "To my brother Ebenezer on his fifth birthday."

If my father was the younger brother, he must either have made some strange mistake, or he must have written, before he was five, a clear and manly style of writing. If he had been older than Ebenezer, then the Shaws should, by law, have come to me as his heir.

When I went back into the kitchen and we sat at table to eat, I asked Ebenezer if my father had been very quick with reading and writing.

"Not him," was the reply. "I was far quicker myself. Why, I could read as soon as he could."

A thought came into my head. "You weren't twins, were you?" I asked.

He was off his stool in a flash, and caught me by the breast of the jacket. "Why do ye ask that?" he said.

For the first time he looked me straight in the eyes.

"What do you mean?" I asked calmly, for I was far stronger than he. "Take your hand from my jacket."

He let go of me. "Ye shouldn't speak to me about your father," he said. "He was the only brother I ever had."

I could not understand him. I began to think that he was mad, and might be dangerous. Then I wondered if he had some cause to fear me.

We sat at table like a cat and mouse, each stealthily watching the other.

"Davie," said my uncle at last, "Here's a bit of money I

half promised your father I'd give ye. It's a matter of" – he paused and stumbled – "of just forty pounds."

I could see that the story was a lie.

"Sir!" I said innocently. "Forty pounds!"

"That's what I said. If you'll step outside a minute, I'll get it out for ye and call ye in again."

I did as he asked, smiling at the way he thought to trick me so easily. It was a dark night, with a few stars. I heard a hollow moaning of wind far off among the hills. There was something thundery and changeful in the weather.

When I was called in again, my uncle counted out into my hand thirty-seven golden guinea pieces. The rest was in his hand in small gold and silver, but his heart failed him there and he crammed the change into his pocket.

"There," he said unhappily, "that'll show you. I'm a man who always keeps his word."

I said that I didn't know how to thank him.

"It's a pleasure to help my brother's son," he said. "But look ye, Davie, I'm growing old and it'd be nice for ye to help me a bit with the house and garden."

I answered that I would do anything to help.

He pulled a rusty key out of his pocket. "There," he said, "that's the key of the stair tower at the far end of the house. Ye can only get into it from the outside, for that part of the house is not finished. I want ye to go up the stairs and bring me down the chest that's at the top. There's papers in it," he added.

"Can I have a light?" I asked.

"No," he answered. "No lights in my house."

"Are the stairs good?" I asked.

"They're grand," he said. "Keep to the wall – there's no banister, but the stairs are grand under foot."

I went out into the night. The wind was still moaning in the distance. The night was black and I had to feel along the wall till I came to the door at the far end of the unfinished wing. I'd got the key in the keyhole and had just turned it, when all of a sudden, there came a brilliant flash of lightning. The sky went black again and I was half-blind as I stepped into the tower.

It was as dark as the pit inside. I groped with hand and foot until I found the wall with the one and the lowermost stair with the other. The steps, though steep and narrow, were regular. I kept close to the tower side and felt my way with a heavily beating heart.

The house stood five storeys high. As I climbed, it seemed that the stairs grew airier and I wondered why.

And then, when I felt sure I was near the top, a second blink of lightning came and went. I stopped with a hoarse cry of alarm. Where the floor should have been there was no floor. There was just empty space.

I was perched on the edge of a great hole that yawned blackly beneath my feet.

Chapter Three
The Queen's Ferry

In that moment fear had me by the throat. There was a stir of bats in the top of the tower, and flying downwards, they sometimes beat about my face and body.

Again the lightning flashed, again I saw the emptiness at my feet. The stair had been carried no higher. Only the lightning had saved me.

My uncle knew what he was doing. He had sent me here to die. I swore I would settle with him for it.

I turned and groped my way down again. The wind sprang up as I went and the rain followed it in buckets.

I went out into the storm and crept into the kitchen. My uncle was sitting with his back to me at the table, a bottle of whisky close to his hand. He seemed to be taken by a fit of deadly shuddering. I saw him lift the bottle to his lips and gulp down the raw spirits.

I stepped forward, came close behind him, and suddenly clapped my two hands down upon his shoulders. "Aah!" I cried.

He started, looked up at me, gave a broken cry like a sheep's bleat, flung up his arms and tumbled to the floor like a dead man. I let him lie as he had fallen. His keys

were hanging in the cupboard, and I wanted some kind of weapon before he came to his senses.

I turned to the chests. The first was full of meal; the second of money bags and papers tied in sheaves; in the third were clothes and a rusty, ugly-looking dagger. This I hid inside my waistcoat.

My uncle still lay as he had fallen. I got water and dashed it in his face. His eyelids fluttered. He looked up and saw me, and there was terror in his eyes.

I sat him on a chair and looked at him. "Why did you try to kill me?" I demanded.

"I'll tell ye in the morning," he said brokenly. "As sure as death I will. Now, let me get to my bed."

He was so weak that I could not keep him. I helped him to his room, locked him in and pocketed the key. In the kitchen, I made up a great fire, wrapped myself in my plaid and fell asleep.

I was awake and up before the last of the stars had vanished and after a plunge in the icy burn, I set my prisoner free.

"Why are you afraid of me?" I blurted out. "Why did you try to kill me?"

He muttered something about a joke and I saw by his face that he was getting ready to lie. I was about to tell him so when there came a knock at the door.

On the doorstep was a half-grown boy in sea-clothes. He winked and made a face at me. "I've brought a letter

from Captain Hoseason to Mr Balfour," he said, and
showed me a letter as he spoke. "And I say, mate," he
added, "I'm awful hungry."

I brought him in and sat him down, where he fell to on
the remains of my breakfast. My uncle, meanwhile, had
read the letter. He got to his feet and pulled me aside.

"Davie," he said, "I've got some business to see to with
this man Hoseason, who's captain of a trading brig, the
Covenant, of Dysart. There's some papers I must sign, and
there's a lot of money in it for you and me. Now, if we
were to walk over to the Queen's Ferry with this lad, I
could see the captain and then we could go on and see
the lawyer, Mr Rankeillor. He knew your father, and
there's something I'd like him to tell ye."

I stood and thought about it. There would be so many
people about at the Ferry that he could do me no harm.
I made up my mind. "All right," I said, "let's go to the
Ferry."

The wind blew straight in our faces. It was June, but it
might have been winter. My uncle was silent, and I was
thrown for talk on the cabin-boy. His name was Ransome
and he had been at sea since he was nine. He boasted of
wild things he had done – theft, piracy, even murder.

I asked him about the ship and of Captain Hoseason.
The ship, he said, was the finest ship that ever sailed,
and the skipper was a man who cared for nothing – he
was rough, fierce and brutal.

"He ain't no seaman, though," the boy admitted. "It's Mr Shuan that navigates the brig. He's a fine seaman, except when he's drunk!" He turned down his stocking and showed me a great, raw, red wound. "He done that – Mr Shuan done it," he said, with an air of pride.

It seemed to me that the brig *Covenant* was little better than a hell upon the seas.

Just then, however, we came to the top of a hill and we all three pulled up and looked down upon the Ferry. Ransome pointed out the *Covenant* anchored offshore.

"What are we standing here for?" my uncle said peevishly. "It's perishing cold. Let's get down to the inn."

The Hawes Inn stands at the end of the pier on the south shore of the Firth of Forth. As soon as we reached it, Ransome led us up the stairs to a small room, heated like an oven by a great coal fire. At a table near the chimney a tall, dark man sat writing. He wore a thick sea-jacket and a tall hairy cap drawn down over his ears.

He got to his feet and came forward. "I'm glad you're here in time, Mr Balfour," he said in a fine, deep voice. "We'll be sailing before dark."

"You keep your room very warm, Captain Hoseason," returned my uncle.

"I've a cold blood, sir," said the skipper. "It's the same with most men who've lived in the tropics."

I was so sickened by the heat that when my uncle told me to "go downstairs awhile", I took him at his word.

I crossed the road in front of the inn, and walked down upon the beach. As I watched the *Covenant* shaking out her sails, a spirit of excitement caught me up and made me think of far voyages and foreign places.

Then it occurred to me that the landlord of the inn was a man of that county and I might do well to make a friend of him. I hurried back and called for a glass of ale.

He brought the ale, looked at me a moment, then asked: "You're no relation of Ebenezer?"

I told him no, none.

"I thought not," he said, "and yet ye have a kind of look of Mr Alexander."

I said: "Ebenezer doesn't seem liked in these parts."

"He's a wicked old man," said the landlord, "and yet he was once a fine young fellow. But that was before the rumour got round about Mr Alexander."

"And what was it?" I asked, my heart beating fast.

"That Ebenezer had killed him," said the landlord.

"And what would he kill him for?" I asked.

"To get the Shaws," answered the landlord. "Why else?"

I stared at him. In that moment I seemed to see it all.

"Was my – was Alexander the eldest son?" I asked.

"Indeed he was," said the landlord. "Why else should Ebenezer have killed him?"

He went away, then, leaving me stunned by my good fortune. If what he had said was true, then the Shaws – the house and its broad lands – were rightly mine.

A minute or two later I heard my uncle calling me. I found him with Captain Hoseason in the road.

"Mr Balfour tells me great things of you," said the captain. "Come on board my ship and drink a cup of ale."

"I'm sorry," I said, "but I'm going with my uncle to see Mr Rankeillor, the lawyer."

"Ay, ay," he said, "your uncle told." He suddenly leaned forward while my uncle's back was turned and whispered: "Take care of the old fox. Come on board – I've got something to tell you, and I'll see no harm comes to you."

My heart gave a leap at the thought that I had found a friend and helper. Followed by my uncle, I let the captain lead me to the boat's skiff lying beside the pier.

We came alongside the ship. Hoseason said that he and I must be the first aboard, and once on deck he slipped his arm under mine and began pointing out the parts of the ship.

"Where's my uncle?" I asked suddenly.

"Ay," said Hoseason grimly, "where is he?"

His manner had changed. I realised that I'd been tricked. I felt I was lost. I ran to the bulwarks. The boat was pulling for the town, my uncle sitting in the stern.

I gave a piercing cry. "Help! help! Murder!"

My uncle turned, his face full of cruelty and terror.

It was the last I saw. Strong hands plucked me away from the ship's side. A thunderbolt seemed to strike me. The deck came up and hit me. I knew nothing more.

CHAPTER FOUR
I Go to Sea

I came to myself in darkness. I was in great pain and bound hand and foot. I could hear a roaring of water. The whole world now heaved giddily up, and now rushed giddily down, and I knew that I was lying bound in the belly of the ship. And then I was sea-sick . . . . I lay there for hours, moaning and groaning, until at last I fell asleep.

I was awakened by the light of a lantern shining in my eyes. A small man of about thirty, with green eyes and a tangle of fair hair, stood looking down at me.

I gave a sob. The man felt my pulse and temples, and began to wash and dress the wound on my scalp. "Cheer up," he said, "the world's not finished yet."

He gave me brandy and water in a tin cup, and left me.

Hours later, I saw the glimmer of the lantern as the trap opened and the man with the green eyes came down the ladder, followed by the captain. Neither said a word; but the first set to and dressed my wound, as before. "He's in poor shape, sir." he said. "He's running a fever. I want him taken out of this hole and put in the forecastle."

"I don't care what you want, Mr Riach," returned the captain. "Here he is, and here he stays."

Mr Riach caught him by the sleeve. "You may have been paid to do a murder," he began.

"What kind of talk is that?" Hoseason cried.

"Talk that you understand," he answered. "I'm paid to be second officer of this old tub and I'm paid for nothing more. I'll not stand by and see this lad die."

Hoseason glared at him, then his face changed. "All right," he said. "Put him where ye please."

He went up the ladder and, even in my state of sickness, I saw two things: that the mate was more than a little drunk, and that he had proved a good friend to me.

Minutes later my bonds were cut, I was hoisted on to a man's back, carried to the forecastle and laid in a bunk.

I lay in the forecastle, as a close prisoner, for some days. The cabin-boy Ransome came in at times, now nursing a bruised limb in silent agony, now raving against the cruelty of Mr Shuan. Of the two mates. Mr Riach was sullen, unkind and harsh when he was sober, and Mr Shuan would not hurt a fly except when he was drunk.

Meanwhile, the *Covenant* was meeting strong head-winds and tumbling up and down against head-seas. There was hard work for all hands. The strain told on the men's tempers and there was a growl of quarrelling all day long.

About eleven o'clock one night a man of Mr Riach's watch came below. I heard him mutter. "Shuan's done for him at last."

We all knew who was meant. Captain Hoseason came

down the ladder. He looked sharply round the bunks, then walked straight up to me. "You," he said, "are to change berths with Ransome. We want ye to serve in the round-house."

As he spoke, two sailors appeared carrying Ransome in their arms. The light of the swinging lantern fell direct on the boy's face. It was as white as wax, and had a look upon it like a dreadful smile. My blood ran cold.

"Run away aft with ye!" cried Hoseason.

There was a high sea running, and I could see the sunset still quite bright. We were now on the high seas between the Orkney and Shetland Islands.

I pushed on across the decks, catching at ropes, and just saved from going overboard by one of the hands, who grabbed me.

The round-house was a big cabin standing a man's height above the decks. Inside were a fixed table and bench, and two berths. Underneath was a store-room, entered by a hatchway in the middle of the deck, where all the best of the meat and drink and the powder were collected. Firearms were set in a rack on one of the walls.

A lamp was burning. It showed me Mr Shuan sitting at the table, a brandy bottle and a tin mug in front of him. He stared at the table before him like one stupid.

He took no notice of me; nor did he move when the captain followed and leant on the berth beside me, looking darkly at the mate. His face was very stern.

Presently Mr Riach came in. He gave the captain a glance that meant the boy was dead as plain as speaking. We all three stood without a word, staring down at Mr Shuan, who just went on staring at the table

All of a sudden he put out his hand to take the bottle. Mr Riach stepped forward swiftly and grabbed it away. "No," he rasped out. "There's been too much drinking on this ship. See what it's brought us to, now!"

As he spoke he tossed the bottle through the door into the sea. Mr Shuan started to his feet, murder in his eyes. The captain leaped towards him. "Sit down!" he roared. "Ye drunken swine, ye've murdered the boy!"

Mr Shuan seemed to understand. He sat down again. "Well," he said, "he brought me a dirty mug."

Hoseason walked up to the first mate, took him by the shoulder, led him across to his bunk, and told him to lie down and go to sleep as if he were speaking to a naughty child. The murderer cried a little, but he obeyed.

"Mr Riach," muttered the captain, "nothing must be said about this night's work. The boy went overboard – that's what the story is. Here, David," he added, "get me another bottle. They're in the locker over there," and he tossed me a key. "Ye'll need a glass," he added to Riach. "It was an ugly thing to see."

That was the first night of my duties; and during the course of the next day I got well into the run of them. I had to serve the meals, and all day long I was kept run-

ning with a drink for one or other of my three masters. At night I slept on a blanket on the deckboards.

Though I was clumsy enough at first, both Mr Riach and the captain were strangely patient with me. As for Mr Shuan, he seemed to have gone out of his mind.

On my second day in the round-house we were alone. All at once he got up, as pale as death, and came close to me. "You weren't here before," he said harshly.

"No, sir," I said, swallowing hard.

"There was another boy," he said, and went and sat down without another word, except to call for brandy.

As the days came and went my heart sank lower and lower. No one had yet told me what was to be done with me, but I'd already guessed for myself. The ship was bound for America, where men could be sold as slaves.

More than a week went by, and ill-luck and ill-weather seemed to follow the ship. At last we were beaten so far south that we were in sight of Cape Wrath.

On the tenth afternoon we were lost in a thick, wet, white fog. I saw men and officers listening very hard over the bulwarks – "for breakers," they said. I felt danger in the air and was filled with excitement.

It was about ten at night. I was serving Mr Riach and the captain their supper, when the ship struck something. My two masters leapt to their feet.

"She's struck!" cried Mr Riach.

"No, " said the captain. "We've run a boat down."

CHAPTER FIVE
The Man with the Belt of Gold

The captain was right. We'd run down a boat in the fog. She'd broken in two and gone to the bottom with all her crew but one.

The captain brought him into the round-house, and he looked cool and unshaken by what had happened. He was small but nimble as a goat. His face was burnt dark by the sun and pockmarked. His eyes were unusually light and had a kind of dancing madness in them. When he took off his greatcoat, he laid a pair of silver-mounted pistols on the table, and he was belted with a great sword.

His clothes were very fine and elegant. He had a hat with feathers, a red waistcoat, breeches of black plush, and a blue coat with silver buttons and silver lace.

"I'm sorry, sir, about the boat," said the captain. "You've lost some good friends, maybe?"

"Ay," said the stranger coolly, "very good friends, they were. They would have died for me like dogs."

I knew by his voice that he was a Highlander.

The captain looked him up and down. "I've been in France, sir," he said slowly. "That's a fine coat you're wearing."

The stranger laid his hand on his pistols. "Oho," he said, "is that how the wind lies?"

"Now, don't be hasty," said the captain. "Ye've a French soldier's coat and a Scotch tongue. Put two and two together – and you get a Jacobite!"

I stared at the stranger wide-eyed. Was he, I wondered, a follower of "Bonnie Prince Charlie" – the young Stuart prince who, at the head of our own Highland clans, had planned his ill-fated invasion of England in 1745? Even now, six years later, Charlie was still the "Darling" of the Highlands, and the Jacobites were rebels in the eyes of King George.

The stranger was smiling at Hoseason. "Well, sir," he said lightly, "I am one of those honest gentlemen that were in trouble about the years forty-five and six. I was on my way to France – there was a ship cruising here to pick me up – but we missed her in the fog. Now, if you can set me ashore in France I'll see that you're well paid."

The captain's eyes gleamed. "I can't land you in France," he said, "but might manage to put ye back where ye came from."

Then he ordered me off to the galley to get supper for the gentleman. When I came back the stranger had taken a money-belt from about his waist and poured a few golden guineas out on the table. The captain was looking at the coins. "Give me half of it," he cried, "and I'm your man!"

The stranger swept the coins back into his belt. "I've told ye," he said, "that it belongs to my chieftain, but there's thirty guineas for ye if ye set me ashore, sixty if ye drop me on the Linnhe Loch."

"Ay?" said Hoseason. "And if I hand ye over?"

"Ye'd be a fool," said the other. "King George's redcoats are in Scotland, trying to wring money out of decent Scots folk. If they get their hands on this, how much of it'll come to you?"

"Well," said the captain, "ye may be right at that. I'll take the sixty guineas, and here's my hand on it."

"And here's mine," said the other.

And thereupon, oddly enough, the captain hurried out and left me alone with the stranger.

I looked at him with a lively interest. "So you're a Jacobite?" I said, as I set meat before him.

"Ay," he said, beginning to eat. "But look here, this brandy bottle of yours is dry. It's hard if I have to pay sixty guineas and then am grudged a drink."

I answered, "I'll go and ask for the key."

The fog was as close as ever, but I saw the captain and the two mates in the middle of the ship, their heads close together. I crept forward very quietly.

"If we go for him in the round-house," I heard Hoseason say, "he hasn't room to use his sword. We can pin him by the arms before he has time to draw."

As I listened, I was filled with fear and anger.

I coughed and stepped forward boldly. "Captain," I said, "the gentleman wants a drink and the bottle's empty. May I have the key?"

They all started and turned about.

"Here's our chance to get firearms!" cried Riach, "David, d'you know where the pistols are kept?"

"David knows," put in Hoseason. "Ye see, David, that wild Highlander is a traitor to King George."

"Yes," I answered, "I know."

"The trouble is," went on the captain, "that all our firearms are in the round-house – and we can't get at them without him seeing. But you could, David. If you can do it, lad, I'll give ye a fistful of his gold."

"All right," I said, a little breathlessly. "I'll do it for you."

"Good lad! Here's the key. Now, mind how you go!"

What was I to do? These men were dogs and thieves; they'd stolen me from my own country; they'd killed poor Ransome. Was I to help them do another murder?

I'd not really made up my mind when I walked back into the round-house. The stranger was sitting with his back to me. I walked right up to the table. "Do ye want to be killed?" I asked quietly.

He sprang to his feet. A hand went to his sword.

"They're all murderers here," I cried. "They've murdered a boy already. Now it's you they're after!"

"Will ye stand by me?" he said.

"That I will!" I answered readily. "I'm not a murderer."

"Good lad!" he said. "What's your name?"

"David Balfour," I answered, and then added, for the first time, "of Shaws."

"My name is Stewart," he said, drawing himself up, "but they call me Alan Breck. Now, tell me what they're planning against me?"

When I'd finished, he looked all round the cabin. It was strongly built and its doors could be drawn close. One was already shut, and I moved to slide the other.

Alan stopped me. "Leave that door open," he said. "As long as it's open my enemies will be in front of me."

He handed me a cutlass then told me to load all the pistols from the rack. He drew his great sword and made a few trial sweeps with it.

"There's not a lot of room," he said regretfully. "How many will there be against us?"

I counted them up in my head. "Fifteen," I said.

"Well," he said, "I'll hold this door, where we shall get the main rush. I want ye to climb up into that bunk, where you'll be close by the window. If they lift a hand against the other door, you're to shoot. What else will ye have to guard?"

"There's the skylight," I said. "But I'd need eyes on both sides to watch window and skylight."

"Lad," Alan said, "have ye no ears to your head?"

"Why, yes!" I cried. "I see what you mean. If they come to the skylight, I shall hear the bursting of the glass."

I'd scarce spoken when the captain showed his face in the open doorway.

Alan swung towards him and light glittered on the naked blade of his sword.

The captain froze. "This is a strange return for kindness," he said.

Alan said proudly, "I bear a king's name and my sword has slashed off the heads of more enemies than you have toes. Call up your rats, and let's begin!"

The captain said nothing, but gave me an ugly look. "I'll remember this, David," he said.

Next moment he was gone.

"He'll be back," said Alan, "and he won't be alone!"

He drew a dagger into his left hand. I clambered up into the bunk with an armful of pistols, and opened the window where I was to watch. The sea had gone down and there was a great stillness in the ship.

There came a clash of steel upon the deck, and I knew that they were dealing out the cutlasses.

My chest was tight, my mouth dry but I was also filled with anger. My wish was to begin and be done with it.

It came with a rush of feet and a roar of hoarse voices. Mr Shuan, sword in hand, appeared in the doorway. Steel clashed on steel. There were grim and scowling faces at his shoulder. I took a long, deep breath.

CHAPTER SIX
The Siege of the Round-House

"Look to your window, David!"

The cabin rang to the clash of steel. I turned to the window only just in time. Five men carrying a small mast ran past me to drive in the closed door. As they swung the yard I cried out: "Take that!" And sent a ball into their midst. There was a cry. A man staggered back. I sent another ball over their heads. At my third shot the whole party ran out of sight.

I swung round. Alan was standing as before. His sword was red to the hilt. On the floor was Mr Shuan. Blood was pouring from his mouth. Two sailors caught him by the heels and dragged him from the round-house. The rest of the crew vanished from sight.

"They'll be back again," Alan said shortly.

I settled back in my place, recharged the three pistols I had fired, and kept watch with both eye and ear. A minute later there came a shrill call on the sea-pipe. A knot of men, cutlasses in hand, made a rush against the door. At the same moment someone kicked in the glass of the skylight. A man leaped through and fell sprawling on the floor. Before he could get to his feet, I clapped a pistol to

his back. He whipped straight round and grabbed for
me, roaring out an oath. I gave a shriek and shot him in
the body. He gave a horrible groan and fell to the floor.

I heard Alan call out. A seamen had caught him round
the body. I saw Alan stab at the man with his left hand,
but the fellow clung like a leech. Another man broke in,
his cutlass raised. The door was filled with savage faces.
I snatched up my cutlass, and fell on them from the side.

Even as I moved Alan smashed the wrestler to the floor.
He leaped back, then ran at the others like a bull, roaring as he went. They broke before him like water, turning and running and falling against one another in their
mad haste. In a moment they were gone.

Alan placed his hands on my shoulders. "David," he
said, "I love you like a brother. And O man," he added,
"am I not a bonny fighter?"

Thereupon he sat down upon the table, sword in hand,
and burst out into a wild Gaelic song.

I staggered to a seat. Suddenly I was filled with horror
at my own share in the fight. I began to sob like a child.

Alan clapped me hard upon the shoulder. "You're a
brave lad," he said. "What you want is a good sleep to
put you right. I'll take the first watch."

I made up my bed on the floor and tumbled on to it.
Alan sat on the table, pistol in hand and sword on knee.
He roused me three hours later, and I took my turn,
waiting for an attack that never came.

It was a quiet morning, with a smooth rolling sea that tossed the ship and made the blood run to and fro on the round-house floor.

On deck nothing stirred. Looking out of the door of the round-house, I saw the great stone hills of Skye on the right and, a little more astern, the strange isle of Rum.

Alan and I sat down to breakfast about six o'clock amidst broken glass and a mess of blood.

As soon as we were seated, Alan took a knife and cut me off one of the silver buttons from his coat. "David," he said, "I'm giving you this as a keepsake for last night's work. Wherever ye go and show that button, the friends of Alan Breck will stand by you."

We'd no sooner finished our meal than we were hailed by Mr Riach from the deck. I climbed through the skylight and sat on the edge of it with a pistol in either hand.

We looked at each other. He had a cut down one cheek. "The captain wants to talk to your friend. They might have a word together at the window."

"And how do we know what treachery he means?" I cried.

"He means none, David," returned Mr Riach. "We couldn't get the men to follow us again if we wished. And I've had enough myself."

I called down to Alan who agreed to speak with the captain. Hoseason came to one of the windows.

Alan pointed a pistol at his head.

"Put that thing down," said the captain. "There'll be

no more fighting. I haven't men enough left to work my ship. There's nothing left for me but to put back into the port of Glasgow after hands. There ye'll find those who are better able to deal with you!"

"Ay?" said Alan lightly. "Well, I'll have a talk with them myself. I've a fine tale to tell – how there were fifteen brave sailors on one side, and a man and a boy upon the other. O man, it'll make all Glasgow laugh."

Hoseason flushed red.

"No," Alan went on, "that won't do at all, captain. Ye'll just have to set me ashore as we agreed."

"How?" said Hoseason. "My first officer is dead and the rest of us don't know this coast."

"Just set me on dry ground, where ye please, within thirty miles of my own country," said Alan.

The captain scowled. "What you want will cost money."

"I'll give thirty guineas if ye land me on the coast," said Alan, "and sixty if ye put me in the Linnhe Loch."

"Could ye pilot us at all?" asked the captain.

"I'm more of a fighting man than a sailor," answered Alan. "But I've been often enough picked up and set down upon this coast."

"If I hadn't lost so much money on this trip," Hoseason said, "I'd see you dangling from a rope's end before I'd risk my ship, sir. But have it as ye will. As soon as I get a puff of wind, I'll try to find my way in."

CHAPTER SEVEN
I Hear of the Red Fox

We sailed in bright sunshine, with many mountainous islands upon different sides. Alan and I sat in the round-house with the doors open on each side. It was then that we heard each other's stories.

Alan said that I should be put ashore with him. "With the redcoats on the look-out for rebels," he said, "ye need to know what you're doing when ye take to the heather."

While I was telling him my own story, I mentioned Mr Campbell, the minister of Essendean. Alan fired up at once and cried that he hated all of that name. "There's only one thing I'd help a Campbell to," he said, "and that's a leaden bullet!"

"But why?" I asked. "Why do you hate the Campbells?"

"Well," he answered, "I'm one of the Appin Stewart clan, and the Campbells have always been our enemies. They've got lands from us by treachery – though never with the sword."

He smashed one fist into the other as he spoke. "David," he said suddenly, "it would be a sorry thing for me if I fell among the redcoats. You ought to know that I was once one of them myself."

"What!" I cried. "Were you in the English army?"

"Ay," said Alan, "but I deserted to Bonnie Prince Charlie's army in forty-five, before the battle of Prestonpans. It would be a long rope for Alan if they got their hands on me."

"Good heavens, man!" I cried. "You're a rebel, a deserter, and a soldier of the French King. Why, then, do ye come back to Scotland?"

"I weary for my friends and country," said Alan. "And then I have a few things that I must attend to – mostly the business of my chief, Ardshiel."

"I thought they called your chief Appin," I said.

"Ay, but Ardshiel is the captain of our clan," he said, and left me none the wiser. "Ye see, David, though he comes of the blood of kings, he now lives in France like a poor man. Now, the tenants of Appin have to pay a rent to King George; but the poor folk scrape up a second rent for Ardshiel. I'm the hand that carries it." He struck the belt about his body so that the golden guineas rang.

"Well, I call that noble!"

"That's because you're a gentleman. Now, if ye were one of the accursed race of Campbell you'd gnash your teeth to hear of it. If ye were the Red Fox . . ." And at that name his teeth shut together.

"And who's the Red Fox?" I asked.

"He is a Campbell, red-headed Colin of Glenure – King George's agent on the lands of Appin. He found out how

the poor men of my clan were sending a second rent overseas for Ardshiel. He swore he'd rid himself of the Stewarts by fair means or foul. He sent for lawyers and papers, and redcoats to stand at his back. With their help, he turned many of the poor people of my clan out of their homes and farms. He's still at it now. He's only one idea – and that's to hurt Ardshiel and the Stewarts."

I said, "Perhaps he's been ordered to do these things. If you killed him tomorrow, there'd be another in his place."

"You're a good lad in a fight," said Alan moodily, "but there are some things you just don't understand."

I asked him how, with the Highlands covered with troops, he was able to come and go without arrest.

"The heather's a great help." he said, "And there are friends' houses, barns and haystacks everywhere. When people talk of a country covered with troops, what does it mean? A soldier covers no more of it than his boot soles. I've fished a stream with a sentry on the other side, and killed a fine trout without his knowing. I've sat in a heather bush within six feet of another, and learned a real bonny tune from his whistling."

After that we both fell silent for a long while.

Late that night Hoseason clapped his head into the round-house door. He looked worried.

He said to Alan, "Come out and see if you can pilot us."

"Is this one of your tricks?" asked Alan.

"Do I look like tricks?" cried the captain. "I've other things to think of – my ship's in danger!"

The sky was clear, though the wind blew hard. The moon, which was nearly full, shone brightly. The hills of Mull lay full upon the larboard bow. The brig was tearing through the seas at a great rate, pitching and straining and chased by a westerly swell. She rose suddenly on the top of a high swell and the captain pointed, crying out to us to look. Away on the lee bow a thing like a fountain rose out of the moonlit sea. Immediately after we heard a low sound of roaring.

"The sea is breaking on a reef," said Alan, "and now ye know where it is. Steer clear of it."

"That would be easy," said Hoseason, "if it was the only one."

Sure enough, just as he spoke, there came a second fountain farther to the south.

"There!" said Hoseason. "If I'd known of these reefs, six hundred guineas wouldn't have made me risk my ship in such a stoneyard."

"These'll be what they call the Torran Rocks," said Alan, "It sticks in my mind that there are ten miles of them."

Mr Riach and the captain looked at each other.

"Is there a way through?" asked the captain.

"I've heard that it's clearer under the land," said Alan.

"So?" said Hoseason. "We'll have to come as near in

about the end of Mull as we can take her, Mr Riach."

He gave an order to the steersman and sent Riach aloft to the foretop. There were only five men on deck, these being all that were fit to man ship.

"The sea's thick to the south," Mr Riach cried. "It does seem clearer in by the land."

"Well, sir," said Hoseason to Alan, "we'll try your way of it. Pray God you're right!"

As we got nearer to the turn of the land, the reefs began to be sown here and there in our very path. Again and again Mr Riach yelled down for us to change course. Once or twice he was none too soon.

The night was so bright that we could see these perils as clearly as by day. Neither the captain nor Mr Riach had shown well in the fighting, but they were brave in their own trade. Alan, on the other hand, was very white.

"David," he said once, "this isn't the death I fancy."

"What!" I cried. "Are you afraid?"

"No," he said, "but it's a cold ending."

By this time we'd got round Iona and begun to come alongside Mull. The tide ran very strong and threw the ship about. Two hands were put to the helm and Hoseason himself would sometimes lend a hand. It was strange to see three strong men throwing their weight on the tiller, while it struggled against them like a live thing.

At last the dangers dropped astern. Mr Riach called from the top that he could see clear water ahead.

Hoseason turned to Alan. "Ye were right," he said. "Ye've saved the ship, sir. I'll remember that when—"

"Keep her away a point!" Riach yelled suddenly "Reef to windward!"

At the same moment the tide caught the brig and threw the wind out of her sails. She came round into the wind like a top. The next moment the ship struck the reef with a tearing crash that threw us all flat upon the deck.

CHAPTER EIGHT
The Loss of the Brig

I was on my feet again at once. The reef we'd struck was off a little isle they called Earraid, which lay low and black upon the larboard. The swell was now breaking clean over us. We could hear the ship grinding upon the reef, beating herself to pieces.

I saw Mr Riach and the seamen busy round the skiff. I ran to help them. It was no easy task, for the breaking of the heavier seas again and again forced us to give over and hold on.

Some of the wounded tried to help. The rest, in their bunks, harrowed me with their screaming to be saved. The captain stood groaning to himself whenever the ship hammered on the rocks. The brig, it seemed, was like wife and child to him.

I asked Alan what country it was. "The worst possible for me," he said grimly. "It's the land of the Campbells."

We had the boat about ready to be launched, when there was a shrill cry: "For God's sake, hold on!"

A huge sea was crashing down on us. It canted the ship right over on her beam. The sudden tilting threw me clean over the bulwarks and into the sea.

I went down, drank my fill, and then came up. I do not know how often I went down, or how often I came up again. All the while I was being hurled along, beaten and choked, and then swallowed whole by the waves.

Then, with a suddenness that was surprising, I was in quiet water. I found that I was clinging to a broken spar. I was amazed to see how far I'd travelled from the ship. She was still holding together.

Between the ship and the clear water in which I floated, I could see the sea boiling white all over. It was the tide race which had carried me away so fast, and then flung the spar and me far in towards the land.

I was a poor swimmer, but I took hold of the spar and kicked out with my feet. It was hard work, but in about an hour I'd got well in between the points of a sandy bay surrounded by low hills and as the water grew shallow I was able to wade ashore.

I was glad to be alive, but never had I seen such a lonely and deserted place.

It was half past twelve in the morning, I guessed, and I was bitter cold. I dared not sit down in case I froze. I took off my shoes and walked to and fro upon the sand, beating my arms wearily. There was no sound but that of the surf, and before long the loneliness of the place struck me with a kind of fear.

As soon as day began to break I put on my shoes and climbed the nearest hill. From the top of the hill I could

see no sign of the ship, which must have lifted from the reef and sunk.

My belly was aching with hunger. I set off eastward along the coast, hoping to find a house.

It was hard to keep walking. The island was nothing but a jumble of rocks with heather in among them. I struggled on until I came to rising ground – and a moment later it burst upon me with the force of an explosion that I was cast upon a little barren isle, and cut off on every side by the salt seas.

It began to rain, with a thick mist, as I stood there. I just shivered helplessly and wondered what to do.

I found plenty of limpets, and those little shells called buckies in Scotland and periwinkles in England. I ate handfuls of them both, cold and raw as I found them. At first I thought them delicious, but as soon as I'd finished my first meal I was seized with giddiness and retching.

On the second day I crossed the island to all sides. Nothing lived on it but birds, which I lacked the means to kill. The island was cut off from the mainland of the Ross by a narrow strait that opened out on the north into a bay, and the bay opened into the Sound of Iona.

I made another meal off the shellfish and managed to keep them down. From the top of a hill I could catch a glimpse of the ancient church and the roofs in Iona. On the other hand, over Ross, I saw smoke go up morning and evening.

In the morning of the third day I saw a red deer, a buck with a fine spread of antlers. He'd scarce seen me rise from under my rock than he trotted off. I supposed that he'd swum across the strait.

I was, by that morning, in a pitiful state. My clothes were beginning to rot. My throat was sore.

As I scanned the sea, all of a sudden a small boat with a brown sail came flying round a rocky point bound for Iona. In it were two fishermen.

I came to my feet. I shouted. I screamed. I fell on my knees and threw up my hands and prayed to them at the top of my voice. They were near enough to hear every word. I could even see the colour of their hair. There was no doubt that they saw me, for they cried out in the Gaelic tongue and laughed. But as I stood there filled with horror and disbelief, the boat never turned aside. It flew on, before my eyes, towards Iona.

CHAPTER NINE
Death of the Red Fox

I ran along the shore, screaming after the pair of them even when they were out of hearing.

Later that day I knew that I was ill. My teeth began to chatter and I had violent fits of shuddering.

The next day I was very weak, but the sun shone and I managed to drag myself to my high rock. No sooner was I there than I saw a boat coming. I ran down to the shore and out from one rock to another as far as I could go.

Still the boat came on. It was the same boat and the same two men. Now there was a third man.

As soon as they were within hailing distance, they let down their sail and lay quiet. I shouted to them again and again, but they drew no closer, and the new man tee-hee'd with laughter.

Then he stood up in the boat and rattled away at me in Gaelic. I shrugged my shoulders and waved my arms to tell him that I did not understand. By listening very carefully, I caught the word "whateffer" several times.

"Whatever," I shouted.

"Yes, yes, yes," he answered and began again in the Gaelic.

This time I picked out another word, "tide". He kept waving towards the mainland of the Ross.

"Do you mean when the tide is out?" I shouted.

"Yes, yes," he answered. "Tide!"

I turned and ran. I'd got his meaning now, and I saw what a fool I'd been.

I leaped from one rock to another, and ran across the little island as I'd never run before. In about half an hour I came out on the shores of a little creek which led out into the strait. It was shrunk into a trickle of water. A few minutes later I landed with a shout on the main island.

I'd starved with cold and hunger for close on one hundred hours; and all I'd had to do, at the right time, was wet my feet.

I set out for the smoke I'd seen so often from the island and came upon a house in the bottom of a little hollow about five in the afternoon. On a mound in front of it, an old gentleman sat smoking his pipe in the sun. With what little English he had, he gave me to understand that Alan and my shipmates had got safe ashore.

"Tell me about the one dressed like a gentleman," I cried eagerly.

"Ah," he said, "you must be the lad with the silver button. A message I have. Follow your friend to his own country, by way of Torosay."

He took me into the house, where his wife gave me meat and bread, and a tankard of strong punch. The

punch threw me into a sweat and a deep sleep, and it was near noon of the next day before I took the road.

About eight at night, when I was very tired, I came to a lone house. The man of the house refused to take me in. I groped in my pocket and held up one of the golden guineas that I'd made from the sale of my father's things. The man's face changed. He agreed to give me a night's lodging and to guide me the next day to Torosay.

Next morning my host led me out upon the road.

No sooner had we crossed the first hill than he told me that Torosay lay right in front, and that a hill-top, which he pointed out, was my best landmark.

"Does it matter," I said, "if you are going with me?"

He stood still, shrugging his shoulders and saying in Gaelic that he had no English. I glared at him.

"So your English comes and goes," I said. "Tell me what will bring it back. Is it more money you want?"

"Five shillings more," he said, "and I'll take ye there."

I thought about it, sighed, then offered him two, which he grabbed at once. The two shillings, however, only took him a little way. He sat down beside the road and took off his brogues, like a man about to rest.

"Hah!" I said, "have you no more English?"

He grinned. "No," he said.

At that I boiled over, and lifted my hand to strike him. He snatched a knife from his rags. I darted in, struck aside his knife with my left, and hit him hard in the mouth

with my right. He went down heavily before me, and his knife, by good luck, flew out of his hand as he fell.

I snatched up the knife and his brogues and set off.

I came, some hours later, to Torosay, on the Sound of Mull. I found an inn, whose landlord spoke good English. I drank punch with him and tried him, as if by accident, with a sight of Alan's button. It was plain that he had never seen or heard of it.

In the morning I went down to the shore of the Sound to take the ferry from Torosay to Kinlochaline. The skipper of the ferry-boat, I'd been told, was called Neil Roy MacRob; and since Alan himself had sent me to the ferry, I was eager to have a word or two with Neil Roy.

I had to wait. It wasn't until he was standing on the beach at Kinlochaline that I was able to get him on one side.

"I'm looking for someone and you may have news of him," I added, and showed him the silver button.

"So you're the lad, are ye?" he said. "I can tell ye what to do next . . . ."

I was to lie the night at the public inn of Kinlochaline, to cross Morven the next day to Ardgour, and stay the night in the house of John of the Claymore, who had been warned that I might come. On the third day, I was to be taken across one loch at Corran and another at Ballachulish, and then ask my way to the house of James of the Glens, at Aucharn in Duror of Appin.

I had some other advice from Neil: to speak with no

one; to avoid Campbells and the "red soldiers"; and to lie in a bush if I saw any of them coming.

I set out on my journey early the next day and had not gone far when I fell in with a stout, solemn man who said his name was Henderland, and who was travelling to Kingairloch. I walked with him, and told him I was going to Ballachulish. I asked him idly if he knew anything about the Red Fox and the Appin tenants.

"Ay," he said, "it's a sorry business, all told. And now Colin Campbell, the King's agent, is turning them out by force. It's started at Duror, and it's there that James Stewart, him they call James of the Glens, is captain of the clan. He's a half-brother of Ardshiel. And then there's one they call Alan Breck. He's a wild man, here today and gone tomorrow – a bold customer, and James's right-hand man."

Mr Henderland asked me to stay the night in his house, standing alone close to the shore of the Linnhe Loch.

The next day Mr Henderland found me a man who was to cross the Linnhe Loch that afternoon into Appin, fishing. He agreed to take me with him.

It was near noon before we set out. The mountains were high and rough, very black and gloomy in the shadow of the clouds, but all silver-laced with streams where the sun shone upon them.

A little after we'd started, the sun shone upon a little moving clump of scarlet close in alongside the water to

the north. Every now and then there came little sparks, as though the sun had struck upon bright steel.

"The red soldiers," said my boatman grimly. "They're coming from Fort William, against the poor people."

At last he set me ashore under the wood of Lettermore close to my secret destination. A bridle-track ran north and south through it. By the edge of it there was a spring, and I sat down beside it to think upon my situation.

Should I join myself with an outlaw like Alan, or should I tramp back to the south country?

And then, the sound of men and horses came to me and I saw four travellers come into view around a turn in the track. They came on one by one and led their horses by the reins. The first was a red-headed gentleman, flushed of face and carrying his hat so that he might fan himself with it. The second, by his black suit and white wig, I took to be a lawyer. The third was a servant and the fourth I knew at once to be a sheriff's officer.

I'd no sooner seen these people than I made up my mind to go through with my adventure. When the first came alongside, I asked him the way to Aucharn.

He stopped and stared at me a little oddly, then turned to the lawyer. "Mungo," he said, "here I am on my road to the job you know about – and here's a young lad who asks if he's on the way to Aucharn."

"Glenure," said the other in a thin voice, "I don't like the look of it. We must be careful."

I gaped at the man with red hair. This, then, was Red Fox – this was Campbell of Glenure, the arch-enemy of the Stewart clan.

He was eyeing me up and down. "And what do ye want in Aucharn?" he asked.

"The man that lives there," I answered.

"James of the Glens," said Glenure, then turned to the lawyer. "Is he gathering his people, think ye?"

"We'd better stay where we are till the soldiers come up," said the lawyer uneasily.

"You've no need to worry about me," I said. "I'm an honest subject of King George."

"Why, that's very well said," replied the Red Fox, "but why are ye seeking the brother of Ardshiel? I have power here, and I have twelve files of soldiers at my back."

"I've heard it said," I answered a little hotly, "that you're a hard man to deal with."

"Well," he said, "your tongue is bold enough." Even as he spoke there came the sound of a shot. He gave a cry and pitched down upon the road.

The lawyer knelt and held him in his arms, while the servant stood moaning. The wounded man looked from one to the other with scared eyes. "Take care of yourselves," he gasped. "They—they've killed me!"

He gave a sigh, his head rolled on his shoulder, and he passed away.

The lawyer's face was as white as the dead man's; the

servant broke out noisy crying. I stood staring at them in horror. The sheriff's officer had run back at the sound of the shot to hasten the coming of the soldiers.

I came to my senses. I began to scramble up the hill, crying out: "The murderer! after the murderer!"

I rushed on. I could see part of the open mountain. A man was running across it. He was a big man, in a black coat, with metal buttons, and carried a fowling-piece.

"There!" I shouted. "I can see him!"

The murderer gave a little, quick look over his shoulder, then began to run all the faster. A few seconds later and he was lost in a fringe of birches.

A voice shouted to me from behind. I halted and looked back. The lawyer and the sheriff's officer were standing just above the road, shouting and waving for me to go back. On their left a company of redcoats, muskets in hands, were beginning to straggle out of the lower wood.

"Ten pounds if ye catch that lad," I heard him shout. "He's an accomplice."

The soldiers began to spread out, some of them running, while others put up their rifles to cover me. I stood, gaping and bemused.

And then I almost jumped out of my skin. A voice spoke. "Duck in here among the trees," it said.

I obeyed. As I did so I heard the crashing of muskets. I paid little heed to that. I was gaping now at the man with a fishing-rod in his hand. It was Alan Breck.

CHAPTER TEN
The House of Fear

"Run!" he said, and then set off running along the side of the mountain towards Ballachulish.

I followed him among the birches, now stooping behind low humps, now crawling on all fours.

The pace was deadly. My heart seemed to be bursting against my ribs. Alan every now and then straightened to his full height and showed himself. Each time he did so there came a shout from the soldiers.

He stopped a quarter of an hour later, clapped down flat in the heather, and turned to me.

"Now," he said, "we've finished playing with them. Do as I do, for your life."

With far more caution, we traced back across the mountainside, only just a little higher. At last Alan threw himself down and lay panting like a dog.

I lay beside him like one dead.

He was the first to come round. He rose, went to the border of the wood, peered out, and then returned.

"Well," he said, "that was hard going, David."

I did not answer. I'd seen murder done upon the man whom Alan hated. I could not look him in the face.

"Are you still worn out?" he asked.

"No," I said. "But you and I must part, Alan. I like you well, but your ways aren't mine."

"If ye feel like that, David," he said gravely, "ye'll have to give me some reason for it."

"You know very well that the Red Fox has been murdered," I answered.

He said quietly, "I had no hand in it. If I wanted to kill a man I wouldn't come out with only a fishing-rod."

I sat up and stared at him. "But do you know who did it? Do you know that man in the black coat?"

"I thought it was blue," replied Alan cunningly.

"Did you know him?" I insisted.

"I couldn't see his face," he answered. "And I've a grand memory for forgetting, David."

"But you showed yourself to the soldiers to draw them after you," I said.

"Well," said Alan, "that was the least we could do for the lad. It'll go hard with him if he's caught. And for us, my lad! We'll have to flee the country. This is a Campbell that's been killed – and if they lay hands on me I'll be tried in Inveraray, the Campbells' head-place. And now you're in it with me, David. We must go together."

"Where can we go?" I asked.

"Down to the Lowlands," he answered. "Mind you, you must always do as I say. But ye've no other chance, Davie, lad. Either take to the heather with me, or else hang."

"I'll go with you," I said, and we shook hands on it.

"Now let's take another look at the redcoats," said Alan, and led me to the north-eastern fringe of the wood.

Far off, wee red soldiers were dipping up and down over the hills and growing smaller every minute.

"They'll be tired before they reach the end of that road," he said. "You and I, David, can strike for Aucharn and the house of James of the Glens, where I must get my clothes and money to see us on our way."

We set out, and as we went we told each other the story of our adventures since we had last met.

Alan had seen me clinging to the spar. It was this that made him hope I'd get safely ashore, and made him leave those clues and messages.

Those still on board the ship had got the skiff launched, and one or two were on board of her already, when there came a second wave, greater than the first, and all who were on deck tumbled one after another into the skiff and fell to their oars. They were not two hundred yards away when there came a third great wave. The ship was lifted clean over the reef, then began to settle down and down. The sea closed over the *Covenant* of Dysart.

No one spoke as they pulled ashore, but as soon as the boat grated on the beach, Hoseason ordered his men to seize Alan. He was like a fiend, shouting that Alan had made them lose their ship, and that it was now their chance to take their revenge. It was seven against one.

"And then," said Alan, "Riach cried out to me to run, and I ran. The last I saw of them, they were all in a knot upon the beach. Fists started going and it seemed better not to wait. I put my best foot forward and sped on my way."

Night fell as we walked and the way we went was over rough mountainsides. I had no idea of how Alan found his way.

At last, at about half-past ten, we came to the top of a slope and saw lights below us. A house door was standing open and all around people were moving hurriedly, each carrying a lighted brand.

Alan whistled three times. At the first shrill sound the moving torches came to a halt. At the third the bustle began again. We went down and were met at the yard gate by a tall, handsome man of more than fifty.

"James Stewart," said Alan, "here is a young gentleman of the Lowlands, who has proved a good friend to me and who is a laird in his own country."

James of the Glens gave me a friendly greeting.

"This shooting," he cried to Alan, "will bring trouble on the whole country. The redcoats will search every house. We're hiding all the arms we possess."

"The Red Fox is dead," said Alan. "Be thankful."

"I wish he was alive again," cried James. "Who's to bear the blame for it? It happened in Appin, and it's Appin that will have to pay."

I looked about me at the servants. Some were on ladders, digging in the thatch of the house or the farm buildings, bringing out guns and swords, while others carried them away. The faces in the torch-light were those of men in a panic.

A girl came out of the house carrying a bundle.

"What's that the lassie has?" asked Alan.

"We're just setting the house in order, Alan," said James "They'll search Appin with candles. We're digging the guns and swords into the moss. The bundle will be your own French clothes. We're going to bury them."

"Bury my French clothes!" cried Alan. "You're not!"

He snatched the bundle from the girl's arms, then went over to one of the barns to dress himself. James led me into the kitchen and sat down with me at table. He was still in something of a fright, like every other soul in the house. His wife sat by the fire and wept; his eldest son crouched on the floor, burning papers in the fire; and a servant girl was searching about the room in a blind hurry.

James rose and began to stride about the room. "I can think of nothing but this dreadful shooting," he said, "and the trouble it's likely to bring."

I was glad when Alan came back, dressed in his fine French clothes. I was given that change of clothing of which I had stood so long in need.

James gave Alan and me a sword and pistol each, some ammunition, a bag of oatmeal, an iron pan and a bottle

of French brandy. We were ready for the heather. Only money was lacking. I still had a guinea or two in my belt. Alan's money-belt had been sent off by another messenger, and he had no more than seventeen pence. As for James, he said that he could only scrape together three-and-five pence halfpenny.

"This won't do," said Alan, frowning.

"This is no time to wait for a guinea or two," said James. "They're sure to be after ye, and ye'll be blamed for to-day's shooting. If they find ye here—" he paused, his face white and drawn. "It's a sorry thing if I'm to get the blame."

"Ay," said Alan slowly, "I see that."

"Ye'll both have to get clear of the country, Alan, for I'll have to offer a reward for the pair of ye to prove that I'm innocent."

"This is a bit hard on the lad," Alan said. "It's like making me a traitor to him."

"Look things in the face," cried James. "There'll be a reward for him and I've got to think of my family."

Alan looked at him for a long moment, and did not seem to like what he saw. He turned to me. "Come on, David," he said. "We'd best be on our way."

We went out into a fine, dark night.

We began to travel over much the same broken country as before. Sometimes we walked, sometimes we ran. For all our hurry, day began to come in while we were

still far from any shelter. We were in a wild valley, strewn with rocks, through which ran a foaming river. Wild mountains stood around it, and I've thought that it might have been called Glencoe, where the Macdonalds were massacred.

"This is no fit place for you and me," he said. "This is a place they're bound to watch."

He ran down to the waterside, to a part where the river was split into two among three rocks. The water poured through the gaps with a horrid thundering. Alan jumped clean upon the middle rock and fell on hands and knees. A moment later and I had followed.

There we stood, side by side, on a small rock slippery with spray, a far broader leap in front of us and the river dinning upon all sides. I could not face that jump. I put my hand over my eyes. Alan shook me. His face was red with anger and he set the brandy bottle to my lips and forced me to drink, which sent the blood into my head again.

"Hang on or drown!" he shouted, then leaped over the farther branch of the river and landed safe.

I was now alone on the rock. The brandy was singing in my ears and I had the sense to see that if I did not leap at once, I should never leap at all. I crouched and threw myself forward. It was only my hands that reached the full length. These slipped, caught again and slipped once more. I was slithering back into the rushing stream when

Alan seized me by the hair and collar and dragged me into safety.

He set off running again for his life. I staggered to my feet and ran after him. I was tired, sick and weary, but I kept stumbling on until at last Alan paused under two great tall rocks that leaned together at the top. You would have said that the man wasn't born who could climb them. Even Alan failed twice in the attempt. It was only at the third trial, and then by standing on my shoulders, that he found a handhold. He scrambled up, let down his leather belt, and with the help of that and a pair of shallow footholds in the rock, I scrambled up beside him.

The two rocks were hollow on the top and sloped one towards the other, making a kind of dish, where as many as four men might have lain hidden.

Alan clapped flat down, and keeping only one eye above the edge, he scouted all round the compass. He smiled.

"Ay," he smiled, "now we have a chance." He looked at me. "You're no great hand at jumping," he said.

I felt myself go red in the face.

"Hoots," he said. "To be afraid of a thing and yet to do it, is what makes the best kind of man."

He went on "I've shown myself a fool this night, David. First I took a wrong road – and that in my own country. Next, I've come without a water bottle, and we must lie here for a long summer's day with nothing but brandy to drink."

"If you'll pour out the brandy," I said, "I'll run back to the river and fill the bottle."

"It's too risky," he answered. "We may have got here only just in time. From sunrise to sunset they'll be hunting us high and low. And now we've talked enough. Go to sleep, lad, and I'll keep watch."

I was only too glad to do as he said. The last thing I heard was the crying of eagles above me.

I was roughly wakened. I started up, with Alan's hand pressed hard upon my mouth.

"Not a sound," he whispered. "You were snoring."

"Well," I muttered, "and why not?"

He signed to me to peer over the edge of the rock.

I took one look and ducked back again. At that one glance I had seen that the valley was full of soldiers.

CHAPTER ELEVEN
The Flight in the Heather

I raised my head and peeped again. It was now high day. About half a mile along the river was a camp of red-coats. A big fire blazed in their midst, at which some of them were cooking. Near by, on the top of a rock nearly as high as ours, there stood a sentry, the sun sparkling on his arms. All the way along the riverside were posted other sentries. Higher up the glen there were horse sol-diers riding to and fro. Lower down there were footmen searching among the heather.

"Ye see," whispered Alan, "this was what I was afraid of, Davie – that they would watch the riverside. But if they'll only keep in the foot of the valley, when night comes, we'll have a shot at getting by them."

"And what are we to do till night?" I asked.

"Lie here," he said, "and bake!"

He was right about that. We lay there on the bare top of the rock like scones upon a griddle.

The long, hot hours passed. We had no water, only raw brandy for a drink, which was worse than nothing.

The soldiers kept stirring all day. We could see the foot-men poking their bayonets among the heather, which

sent a cold thrill into my vitals. They would sometimes hang about our rock so that we scarce dared breathe.

The pain of these hours upon the rock grew only greater as the day wore on. About two in the afternoon we could stand it no longer. The sun had now got round a little to the west, and there was a patch of shade on the side of our rock sheltered from the soldiers.

"We might as well die one death as another," said Alan.

He slipped over the edge of the rock and dropped to the ground on the shadowy side. I followed him, so weak and giddy, that I instantly fell flat on my face.

We lay still for an hour or two, aching from head to foot, and presently we began to feel stronger. Alan suggested that we should try to get away without waiting for night to come and we began to slip from one rock to another, now crawling flat on our bellies, now making a run for it, heart in mouth.

The redcoats had already searched this side of the valley and now, in the heat of the afternoon, stood dozing at their posts or only kept a look-out along the river.

No voice challenged us. We kept down the valley and made at the same time towards the mountains.

I felt that I needed a hundred eyes to keep hidden in that uneven country and within cry of so many scattered sentries. The afternoon was so still that the rolling of a pebble sounded like a pistol shot.

By sundown we had covered a fair distance, though the

sentry on the rock was still plainly in our view. But then we came on something that made us forget all our fears – a deep, rushing stream that tore down a slope to join the river. We threw ourselves beside it, plunged head and shoulders in the water, and drank greedily. Then we mixed some of our oatmeal with cold water and made a kind of porridge in the iron pan.

We set off again as soon as night had fallen. The moon rose and found us still on the road, and it was still dark when we reached our destination, a cleft in the head of a great mountain, with a stream running through, and a shallow cave in the rock at one side. Birches grew there and, farther on, pines.

We stayed there five days. We slept in the cave, making our beds of heather and covering ourselves with Alan's greatcoat. There was a low hidden place in a turning of the cleft, where we dared to make a fire. With that we could warm ourselves when the clouds set in and grill the little trout that we caught with our hands.

Alan gave me lessons in the use of the sword. He stormed at me all through the lessons, and though I could never please him, I was not displeased with myself.

We made plans for our escape from Appin.

"We must get word sent to James, and he must find money for us." Alan said

"How can we do that?" I asked.

"David," said Alan, "I'll find a way. You'll see."

He sat staring into the fire. Presently he took a piece of wood and shaped it into a cross; the four ends he blackened on the coals.

"Could ye lend me my button?" he asked a little shyly. "I don't want to cut off another."

I gave him the button. He strung it on a strip off his greatcoat which he had used to bind the cross, tied it in a little sprig of birch and another of fir.

"Now," he said, "there's a little village not far from here where live friends I could trust with my life and some that I'm not so sure of. There'll be a price on our heads by now. I'll steal down in the darkness and leave this little cross in the window of a good friend of mine called John Breck MacColl. The cross is a signal of gathering in our clan, yet he'll know well enough the clan is not to rise. Then he'll see my button and know Alan Breck is in the heather and has need of him."

"There's a lot of heather between here and the Forth," I said.

"John Breck will see the sprig of birch and the sprig of pine." said Alan. "He'll know I'm in a wood which is of both pines and birches. There aren't so many of those hereabouts, and he'll come up here to find us."

So that night Alan set the little cross in John Breck's window. He was troubled, for the dogs had barked and the folk had run out from their houses. He thought, also, that he'd seen a redcoat come to one of the doors.

Next day about noon we saw a man straggling up the open side of the mountain. Alan gave a shrill whistle, and kept on until the man was guided to us.

He was a ragged, bearded man, about forty, and seemed to be both sullen and afraid.

Alan told him what we wanted.

"No," the man said, shaking his head. "You must give me a letter or I will not do this for you."

We had no pen or paper. But Alan found a quill, which he shaped into a pen; made himself a kind of ink with gunpowder from his horn and water from the stream; and tearing a corner from his French military commission, he wrote:

'Dear Kinsman,
    Please send the money by the bearer
    to the place he knows of.
        Your affectionate cousin,
            A. S.'

Three days later, in the evening, we heard a whistling in the wood, which Alan answered. In a little while John Breck was giving us the news of the country.

It was alive with redcoats, he said. Arms were being found and poor folk falling into trouble. James had been clapped into prison at Fort William, under suspicion of having had a hand in the death of the Red Fox. But it was being said Alan Breck had fired the shot, and there

was a reward of one hundred pounds offered both for him and me.

The note from James's wife begged Alan not to let himself be caught or both he and James would hang. The money she had sent was all that she could beg or borrow. She enclosed one of the reward bills in which we were described.

They'd put Alan down as "a small, pockmarked, active man of thirty-five, dressed in a feathered hat, a French side-coat of blue with silver buttons, a red waistcoat, and breeches of black cloth".

I was described as "a tall strong lad of about eighteen, wearing an old blue coat, very ragged, an old Highland bonnet, a long homespun waistcoat, blue breeches; his legs bare, low-country shoes, wanting the toes; speaks like a Lowlander and has no beard".

We looked at each other and grinned.

"Alan," I said, "you should change your clothes."

"I've no others," he answered.

John Breck gave us a green purse with four guineas in gold, and the best part of another in small change. On this, Alan had to get to France, and I, with less than two already on me, to Queensferry.

We shook hands with John Breck, who took himself off by one way and we another.

We travelled hard for about seven hours. Morning brought us to a piece of low, broken desert land, which

we now had to cross. We sat down in a hollow, made a dish of porridge and held a council of war.

"David," said Alan, "we daren't stay here in Appin. To the south it's all Campbells. There's not much to be gained by going north. That only leaves the east."

"Let's go east, then," I said, quite cheerfully.

"But to the east we have the moors. Out there, where it's all open, where can we hide? It's a bad place, David, though worse by daylight."

"Alan," I said, "it's all a risk. I give you my word to go on until I drop, no matter what happens."

"David," he said, "there are times when I love you like a brother. The moors it is!"

Much of the moorland was red with heather; the rest was broken up with bogs and peaty pools; but it was clear of redcoats.

We went down into the waste and struck off to the east. There were the tops of mountains all round from which we might be spied, so we had to keep in the hollow parts of the moor. Sometimes we crawled from one heather bush to another. The sun blazed down; our water was soon gone.

Toiling and resting and toiling again, we wore away the morning. About noon we lay down in a thick bush of heather to sleep. Alan took the first watch, and it seemed to me that I'd hardly closed my eyes before I was being shaken up to take my turn.

Alan stuck a sprig of heather in the ground to serve as a sundial, so that as soon as the shadow of the bush should fall so far to the east, I might know it was time to rouse him. I was so tired that every now and again I would give a jump and find I had been dozing.

The last time I woke, I thought the sun had taken a great leap in the heavens. I looked at the sprig of heather, and I knew that I'd betrayed my trust. I looked out and my heart almost died. I saw a troop of horse soldiers drawing near, spread out in the shape of a fan and riding their horses to and fro in the heather.

I grabbed for Alan's shoulder and shook him hard.

He took one glance at the soldiers, then up at the sun. I saw him knit his brows.

"We'll have to play at being hares," he said.

He pointed to a mountain to the north-east.

"We'll strike for that. Its name is Ben Alder. It's full of hills and hollows, and if we can get to it before morning we may escape yet. Come on, Davie, be quick!"

He began to run forward on his hands and knees, winding all the time in and out of the lower parts of the moorland, where we were best hidden.

More than once we reached a big bush of heather, where we lay and panted and, putting aside the leaves, looked back at the dragoons. They were holding straight on, beating the ground as they rode. I'd awakened just in the nick of time.

I could hear Alan's breath begin to whistle in his throat. More than once I was ready to give up.

At last, as dusk began to fall, we heard a trumpet sound and, looking back, saw the troop beginning to collect. Later we saw that they had built a fire and camped for the night.

"We'll have no sleep tonight," said Alan. "We got through in the nick of time and we mustn't lose what we've gained. When day comes it should find you and me in a fast place on Ben Alder."

"I can't go on," I said. "I haven't the strength."

"Very well," said Alan. "I'll carry you."

I saw that he meant it and I was filled with shame.

"Lead on," I said heavily. "I'll follow."

It grew cooler with night. Heavy dew fell and drenched the moor. We went on and on, until each step became an agony. Day began to come in, and by then we were past the greatest danger.

Then it happened.

We were going down a heathery slope, when there came a rustle in the heather and three or four ragged men leaped out. The next moment we were lying on our backs, each with a dagger at his throat.

CHAPTER TWELVE
Cluny's Cage

I lay looking up in the face of the man who held me. He was burned nearly black by the sun and his eyes were very light. I don't think I really cared about what had happened. The pain of this rough handling was quite swallowed up by the pains of which I was already full. I heard Alan and another man muttering in the Gaelic.

Our weapons were taken away, and we were allowed to sit up. Alan clapped me on the back.

"They're Cluny's men," he cried. "These sentries will tell their chief that I'm here."

Cluny Macpherson, I knew, had been one of the leaders of the great rebellion six years before. There was a price on his life. I'd supposed him long ago in France.

"What!" I cried. "Is Cluny still here?"

"Ay," said Alan. "Still in his own country and kept by his own clan. Now, I'd like to get some sleep."

He rolled on his face and seemed to sleep at once.

I tried to do the same, but I'd no sooner closed my eyes than my body and my head seemed to be filled with whirring grasshoppers. I had to open my eyes again at once, and tumble and toss, and sit up and lie down again.

That was all the rest I had till the messenger returned. Cluny, it seemed, would be glad to receive us. We must get once more upon our feet. I'd been dead-heavy before, but now I felt a dreadful lightness. The ground seemed like a cloud and a sort of horrid despair sat on my mind.

I saw Alan frowning anxiously. I smiled and could not stop smiling. I heard Alan speak sharply and two of Cluny's men took me by the arms and carried me into the heart of that dismal mountain of Ben Alder.

We came at last to the foot of a steep wood, which scrambled up a scraggy hillside, and was crowned by a naked cliff.

We struck up the hill. The trees clung to the slope like sailors on the shrouds of a ship. Their trunks were like the rungs of a ladder by which we mounted.

At a point just before the rocky face of the cliff sprang above the treetops, we found that strange house which was known as "Cluny's Cage". The trunks of several trees upheld a roof of twigs. The walls were of wattle and covered with moss. The whole house had something of an egg shape and it half hung, half stood in that steep hillside thicket like a wasp's nest in hawthorn. A fire burned in a chimney in the cliff and the smoke rising against the face of the rock, being much the same colour, would easily escape notice below.

We went in. Cluny, the outlawed chief, was seated by

the rock chimney. He had a knitted nightcap drawn down over his ears and was smoking a foul old pipe. He rose, however, with the manner of a king.

"Well, Mr Stewart, come in, sir," he said. "And your friend – whom I have not yet the honour of knowing."

"I'm proud to see ye, Cluny," said Alan, "and to present to ye my good friend, Mr Balfour of Shaws."

"Ye're both welcome to my house," said Cluny grandly. "It may be a queer, rude place but it's where I once entertained a royal person, Mr Stewart – and you'll no doubt know the person I mean. Now, we'll drink together, and as soon as this handless man of mine has the meat cooked, we'll eat as gentlemen should."

He poured brandy into three glasses. "Here's a toast for ye," he said. "The Restoration!"

We all touched glasses and drank. I drained the brandy and at once felt much better.

Cluny, it seemed, was still a great chief in the land, even though he was a hunted outlaw. When he was angry, he gave commands and breathed threats of punishment like any king.

We fed that day on thick slices of venison, cooked to a turn, though I found that I could eat but little. While we were eating, Cluny entertained us with stories of Prince Charlie's stay in the Cage. When the meal was done, Alan suggested that I should rest and Cluny pointed out to me a bed of heather in a corner of the Cage.

I lay down, gladly, and at once a strange heaviness came over me. I fell into a kind of nightmare. Sometimes I knew what was happening around me; sometimes I only heard voices or the sound of men snoring.

Whenever I opened my eyes I saw Alan and Cluny playing cards together. I remember seeing a pile of as much as sixty guineas on the table. It seemed strange to me for Alan to play for money when I knew that he had only five pounds in his purse.

Next day when I awoke, Alan was stooping over my bed. He asked me to lend him my money.

"But why?" I said.

"Now, come, David," he answered, "ye won't begrudge me a little loan?"

I was too sick to argue. I handed him my money.

I woke on the morning of the third day feeling in much better health. I rose from my bed, ate a good breakfast, and sat all morning outside. When I went inside, Cluny and Alan were questioning one of Cluny's wild Highlanders. Cluny turned to me.

"My scout says that all is clear in the south," he said. "Have ye the strength to travel?"

I saw cards on the table, but no gold. Alan had an unhappy look. I knew that something was wrong.

"I don't know if I'm as well as I should be," I said. "The little money we had was to take us a long way."

Alan bit his lip and looked at the ground.

"David," he said, "I've lost it – and that's the truth."

"My money, too?" I asked.

"Your money, too," said Alan. "Ye shouldn't have given it to me. I'm daft when I get to the cards."

"Hoot-toot," said Cluny grandly, "of course you'll have your money back again!"

He began to pull gold out of his pocket. Alan said nothing, only stared at the ground. There was a little silence.

"My friend fairly lost this money," I said, "but can I take it back again? You can see that it's a hard thing for a man of pride to do. But we need it so badly."

"Mr Balfour," said Cluny, "I've no wish to see any friends of mine suffer through the cards. Take the money – and here's my hand along with it!"

I shook hands with him, humbly and gratefully.

That night, Alan and I were put across Loch Errocht and went down its eastern shore to another hiding place near the head of Loch Rannoch. We said nothing as we walked. Alan was ashamed that he had lost my money, and angry that I felt so hurt because I'd had to ask for it back.

At last, Alan could bear it no longer and came close to me. "David," he said, "I have to say that I'm sorry. And now if ye have anything to say, ye'd better say it."

"I've nothing to say," I answered.

"I've said I was to blame," he said harshly.

"Of course you were to blame." I answered.

"David," he said quietly, "I owe you my life, and now I owe you money. But we'll say no more about it."

We fell silent once more.

We crossed Loch Rannoch at dusk of the next day. Then, for the best part of three nights, travelled on eerie mountains and along wild rivers. Never once were we cheered by a glimpse of the sun. Our food was cold porridge and mouthfuls of dried meat from the Cage.

It was a dreadful time. I was never warm; my teeth chattered in my head; my throat was sore.

Still we said little to each other. I was sick again and it seemed to fill me with anger against my friend. For two days he was very kind, while I nursed my anger and looked at him as if he were a bush or a stone.

Dawn of the third day found us on a very open hill, far from shelter and caught in a heavy rain.

"Ye'd better let me take your pack," Alan said, for about the ninth time since we'd left the Cage.

"I'll carry it myself," I answered, as cold as ice.

"I shan't offer again," he said shortly.

That night it was clear and cold. Alan seemed in good spirits and whistled quietly to himself. I was full of pains and shiverings. I felt I could drag myself only a little farther.

Then Alan began to drive me on with taunts and jeers.

"Come on, my fine Lowlander!" he said. "Here's a stream for ye to jump – I know you're a fine jumper."

I staggered on. I knew that he was doing it to keep me going and that had he been kind I should have stopped. But at last I could stand no more. He'd just called me "King George's little man". I stopped and turned on him.

He faced me, smiling in the starlight.

"Mr Stewart," I said, in a voice that quivered like a fiddle string, "from now on you'd better speak kindly of my King and of my good friend Mr Campbell."

"I am a Stewart—" Alan began.

"Oh," I said, "I know that ye bear a king's name. Since I've been in the Highlands I've seen many of that name. The most I can say for them is that they'd be none the worse for a good wash."

"You insult me," said Alan, very low.

"I do," I answered, "and it seems to me that both the Campbells and King George have beaten ye. You should be man enough to speak of them as your betters."

"There are some things," he said at last, "that can't be passed over."

"If you wish to fight," I answered, "then come on!"

I drew my sword and fell on guard.

"Are you daft?" he cried. "I can't fight *you*, David. It would be murder."

"That remains to be seen," I answered. "Come on, draw your sword!"

He drew his sword. I stepped forward. But before I could touch his blade with mine, he threw it from him.

"No," he kept saying. "I can't do it – I can't!"

All my anger oozed out of me. I remembered all Alan's kindness and courage in the past. At the same time, the pain in my side was like a sword.

"Alan," I said, "if you can't help me, I'll have to die."

He stared at me.

"Help me to a house," I said "I'll die there easier. I've a pain in my side like a red-hot iron."

"Don't say that!" he cried. "Ye'll not die, Davie lad. I should have seen ye were dying on your feet. Lean on me hard. There are friends in Balquhidder. I'll get ye there."

"Alan," I said, "what makes ye so good to me?"

"Well, now," said Alan, "I thought the thing I liked best about ye was that ye never quarrelled – but now I like ye all the better!"

CHAPTER THIRTEEN
End of the Flight

Alan knocked at the door of the first house we came to. It was a risky thing to do when we had no idea who lived there. It was a household of Maclarens we found, where Alan was welcomed. There we rested until I was fit enough to travel again.

We were so short of money that I'd made up my mind to go straight to Mr Rankeillor's – the lawyer at Queensferry – to see if he would help me win all that was rightly mine and then I should have money enough to see Alan off to France.

Alan said that the hunt must now have slackened. We must try to get across the Forth by the Stirling Bridge.

"It's always wisest to go where you're least expected," he said. "The Forth is our trouble. If we try to creep round by its head, it's there that the redcoats will be looking out for us. If we keep straight on to the old Bridge of Stirling, I'll lay my sword we get by unchallenged."

We travelled three nights in a row by easy stages till we saw the whole vale of Stirling beneath us.

"Now," said Alan, "you're in your own land again."

In Allan Water, close to where it falls into the Forth, we

found a little sandy island, overgrown with bushes that would just cover us if we lay flat. Here we made our camp within plain view of Stirling Castle, and heard its drums beating as its soldiers paraded. We were warmed by the sun, the bushes gave us shelter for our heads, we had food and drink in plenty.

At dusk we waded ashore and struck out for the Bridge.

The old, narrow bridge is close under the castle. A few lights shone along the castle front. There seemed to be no guard upon the bridge.

"It looks quiet enough," Alan said, "but we'll lie down here in the ditch and just make sure."

We heard nothing but the washing of the water on the piers of the bridge. At last an old woman came by, hobbling with a stick. She stopped for a moment close to where we lay, then went on towards the bridge. The sound of her steps and the tap of her stick drew slowly away.

"She's bound to be across now," I whispered.

"No," said Alan, "her footstep still sounds hollow."

A second later and there came a cry. "Who goes there?"

We heard the butt of a musket rattle on the stones. It was a sentry, without doubt.

"We'll never get across there, David," said Alan sadly.

We turned and began to crawl away through the fields then struck along a road that led to the east.

"Well," said Alan, "they're not such fools as I took them for. We've still got to get over the Forth."

"But why go east?" I asked.

"If we can't pass the river," he said, "we'll have to see what we can do by the firth."

"But there are no fords on the firth," I said.

"I know," said Alan, "but there's such a thing as a boat."

"And such a thing as money," I answered. "We have neither one nor the other."

"Davie," said Alan, "just leave it to me. If I can't beg, borrow or steal a boat, I'll make one."

"If you leave a boat on the wrong side of the firth," I said, "then all the countryside will be wondering why."

"Man," cried Alan, "if I make a boat, I'll make a body to take it back again!"

We walked all night, and about ten in the morning, we came to the little village of Limekilns. It looked across at Queensferry. I thought of Mr Rankeillor's house on the southern shore. There, I felt sure, wealth awaited me.

We found an inn in Limekilns. There we bought some bread and cheese from a good-looking servant girl. We carried it away to the safety of a wood.

"Davie," Alan said, "did you notice the girl who sold us this?" He tapped the bundle of bread and cheese.

"Yes," I said, "she was a fine-looking girl."

"I'm glad you noticed that," said Alan. "It might get us the boat we want."

"How ?" I began.

"David," he said, "we're going back. I want that girl to

feel sorry for you. I wish you were a bit paler, but you look like a scarecrow."

He turned. I followed him, laughing.

"You may think it funny," he said, "but a bit of play-acting may save the pair of us from the gallows."

When we pushed open the inn door he was half carrying me. The girl stared at us. Alan helped me to a chair and called for brandy, which he fed me in little sips.

"What's wrong with him?" the girl asked.

"Wrong with him?" Alan said bitterly. "He's walked hundreds of miles and slept oftener in wet heather than in dry sheets. It's a wonder he's still alive."

"Has he no friends?" she asked. "I can see that you're both gentlemen."

"Yes," cried Alan, "he has rich friends, if only we can get to them, but if his enemies catch him they'll hang him from a tree."

"Poor lamb," said the girl, then ran from the room and came back at once with a dish of meat pudding and a bottle of strong ale.

"Eat up," she said to us both. "I'll not charge you a penny for it. The inn belongs to my father, and he's gone for the day to Pittencrieff."

We needed no second telling.

"What else can I do to help?" she asked.

"Look here, my lass," said Alan, "If we could only get a boat tonight, to take us over the Forth, and some decent

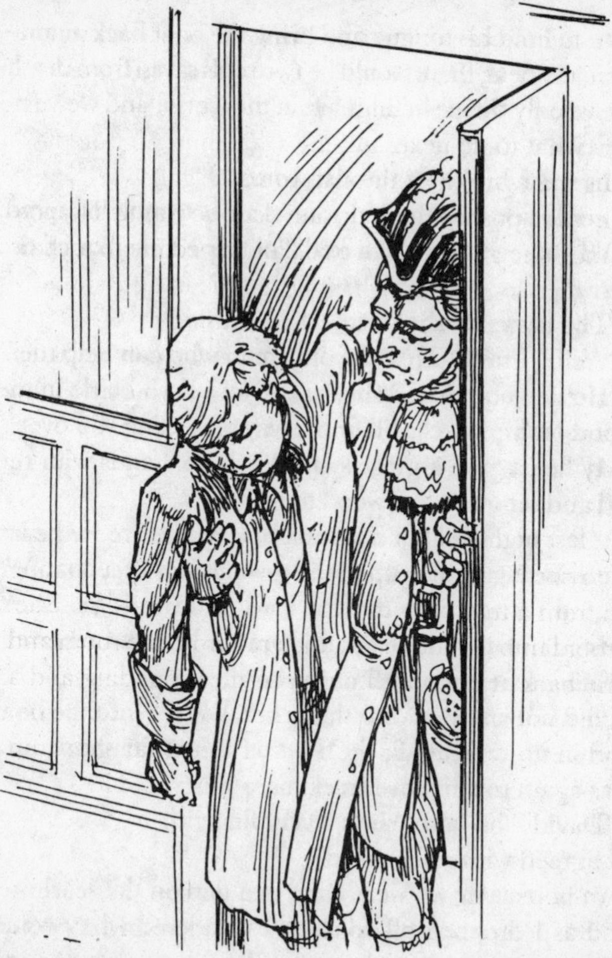

man to hold his tongue and bring the boat back again —
then, my dear, there would be two souls saved from death.
We've only three shillings left in the world, and we've no
idea what to do next."

His voice broke on the last words.

I could see that the girl was in great trouble of mind.
"Did you ever hear," I asked, "of Mr Rankeillor of the
Ferry?"

"The lawyer?" she cried. "Yes, indeed!"

"Well," I said, "He's the only man who can help me."

"He's a good man," she said. "Now, if you hide in the
wood on the beach, I'll find a way of getting you over."

My heart gave a great leap. We shook hands with the
girl and set off to the wood to wait.

At last night fell but it was past eleven before we heard
the grinding of oars upon the rowing-pins of a boat. We
started up and saw the girl rowing towards us. She'd
trusted no one, she said, and come to help us by herself,
stealing a neighbour's boat to do it.

I did not know how to thank her. We got into the boat
and in no time at all, she'd set us on the far shore, and
was again rowing for Limekilns.

"David," he said, "she's a very fine girl!"

I agreed with every word.

An hour later we were lying in a den on the seashore,
and as I dropped off to sleep I wondered what would
happen to me next.

CHAPTER FOURTEEN
The Lawyer

We agreed next day that Alan should stay where he was until sunset. As soon as it grew dark, he would move to the fields by the roadside and wait until he heard me whistling. He taught me a little Highland air which has run in my head from that day to this.

I was in the long street of Queensferry before the sun was up. It was a fairly big town and the fine streets put me to shame for my rags and tatters.

For the life of me I could not nerve myself to speak to any of the townspeople. I was afraid they'd laugh if I asked for the house of such a respectable man as Mr Rankeillor. Up and down I went, sunk in despair.

I began to grow tired. I stopped at last in front of a big house with beautiful clear glass windows and a dog sitting yawning on the step. I saw the door open and out came a ruddy, portly man in a well-powdered wig and spectacles. He stepped out from the door, looked me up and down, came straight to me, and stopped.

"What is it you want?" he asked.

"I'm looking for the house of Mr Rankeillor. I have some business with him," I answered in desperation.

"Well," he said, "that's his house I've just come out of – and I'm the man you're looking for."

"Sir," I said eagerly, "I'm David Balfour. Will you find me the time to talk to you?"

He stared at me, holding his hand to his lip. "You'd best come into the house," he said at last.

He took me into the house and led me into a little dusty room full of books and documents. He looked ruefully from a clean chair to my muddy rags.

"Sit down," he said, "and let's hear what you've got to say. Be as quick as you can."

He gave me a sharp look. My heart leaped within me.

"I believe that I have some claim on the estate of Shaws," I said.

He got a paper book and set it open before him. "Go on, Mr Balfour. Where were you born?"

"In Essendean," I answered, "on the twelfth of March, 1733."

"Who were your father and mother?"

"My father was Alexander Balfour, schoolmaster of that place," I said readily, "and my mother Grace Pitarrow. I think her people were from Angus."

"Have you any papers to prove all this?" he asked.

"No, sir," I answered. "They are in the hands of Mr Campbell, the minister of Essendean, who would readily swear to my identity. For that matter, I don't think my uncle would deny me."

"Meaning Mr Ebenezer Balfour?" he asked.

"Yes."

"Whom you have seen?"

"Who took me into his own house," I answered.

"Did you ever meet a man named Hoseason?"

"He and my uncle had me kidnapped within sight of this town," I cried. "We were shipwrecked and—"

"Where were you shipwrecked?" he asked.

"On the south end of the Isle of Mull," I said.

"H'm! this agrees with other information I've been given. But you say you were kidnapped?"

"I was on my way to your house," I cried, "when I was tricked aboard the ship, cruelly struck down and knew no more till we were far at sea. They were going to take me to America."

"The ship was lost on June twenty-seventh," he said, "and it is now August twenty-fourth – a gap of close on two months."

"Before I tell you my story I must know that you are my friend," I answered. "I can't forget that I was shipped off to be a slave by the very man who is your employer."

"Your uncle *was* my employer," he said drily. "There's been a lot of talk about you, Mr Balfour. On the very day of the shipwreck, Mr Campbell stalked in here and wanted to know where you were. I'd never heard of you, but I knew your father. Mr Ebenezer admitted that he'd seen you; said that he'd given you a large sum of money

and that you had started for Europe. When I stated flatly that I didn't believe him, he showed me to the door. A few days later Captain Hoseason came in with the story of your drowning."

I could see that he took my identity for granted.

"Sir," I said, "I'll tell you my story if you'll promise that anything I say will be sacred."

He gave me his word and I told him my story from the first. When I spoke the name of Alan Breck he stirred in his seat.

"We will call your friend of the Highlands Mr Thomson, if you please," he said. "It will be safer for everyone concerned. This Mr Thomson seems to me a bold and adventurous gentleman, and you should stand by him since he has been your true companion. However, I think you are now near the end of your troubles."

He smiled at me in such a friendly way that I could have cried for joy.

Then my eye fell on my rags and tatters. The lawyer saw and understood. He led me up to a bedroom, set before me water and soap and a comb, laid out some clothes that belonged to his son, then left me.

When I had done, I went down again to his study.

"David," he said, "there are things that I must tell you. It's a strange tale, and one that hinges on a love affair. Your uncle was once a fine-looking young man. So was your father, but unluckily the two of them fell in love

with the same woman. Mr Ebenezer, who was his father's favourite, made sure that he would win her. When
he found that he was wrong, the whole countryside heard
about it. Now, your father was a kind man and hated to
see his brother suffer, and so the two of them made a
sort of bargain. Your father took the lady, who loved him,
and your uncle took the estate of Shaws. So it was that
your father and mother lived and died as poor folk. In
the meanwhile, your uncle, who changed completely,
spent all his time squeezing every penny he could out of
the tenants of Shaws."

"I can't imagine a man would change like that," I said.

"I suppose it was natural enough," replied the lawyer.
"Your father went away and those who saw one brother
disappear and the other succeed to the estate raised a
cry of murder. Everyone gave your uncle the cold shoulder. All he got by his bargain was money."

"Well, sir," I said, "and what is my position in all this?"

"The estate is yours without a doubt," replied the lawyer. "It doesn't matter what your father signed, you are
the heir of entail. But your uncle will fight. If any of your
doings with Mr Thomson were to come out, he'd see
you hanging from the gallows. If it has to come to court,
the kidnapping will be a card on our side, but it may be
difficult to prove. We might find some of the men of the
Covenant who would swear that you had been kidnapped
aboard the ship, but then some word of Mr Thomson

must certainly crop out. I don't think we should let that happen."

"Sir," I said, "this is what I think we should do . . ."

I told him my idea.

"But I'd have to meet this man Thomson," he said when I'd finished. "I don't know if I could do that, when it would be my duty to give him in charge."

"You must be the judge, sir," I answered.

He got a sheet of paper and a pencil and set to work. At last he touched a bell and his clerk entered the room.

"Torrance," he said, "I must have this properly written out at once. When it is done, you will come along with me as a witness."

"Sir," I cried, as soon as the clerk had gone, "are you going to do as I asked?"

"Why, yes, David," he said, "I think I might."

It was almost dusk when we set out from the house, Mr Rankeillor and I, and Torrance following behind with the deed in his pocket and a covered basket in his hand.

We'd passed right out of the town, when Mr Rankeillor clapped his hand to his pockets and began to laugh.

"Why," he cried, "what a madman I am! I've forgotten my glasses, and I'm as blind as a bat without them."

I saw at once that he had done it on purpose, so that he might have the benefit of Alan's help without the awkwardness of recognising him.

As soon as we were past the inn at the Ferry, Mr Rankeil-

lor sent me ahead. I went up the hill whistling my Gaelic
air. I saw Alan rise from behind a bush. One look at my
clothes and his face brightened. I told him quickly what
had happened and what was yet to happen. He clapped
me on the shoulder.

"David," he said, "that's a fine idea – and you couldn't
find a better man to help you than Alan Breck."

I called softly to Mr Rankeillor, who came up alone
and was presented to my friend Mr Thomson.

"I am pleased to meet you," said the lawyer, "but I've
forgotten my glasses and am almost blind. You mustn't
be surprised if I pass you by tomorrow. Now, as you and
I are the chief actors in this enterprise, we should go on
ahead and have a little talk."

Night was come when we came in sight of the house of
Shaws. We saw no glimmer of light in the building. It
seemed that my uncle was already in bed.

The lawyer, Torrance and I crept quietly up and
crouched down beside the corner of the house. Alan
strode up to the door and began to knock.

CHAPTER FIFTEEN
I Come into my Kingdom

For some time Alan's knocking only roused echoes. I could see him, like a dark shadow on the steps, waiting. Then I heard a window being opened.

"What's this?" I heard my uncle call, his voice all shaky. "What do ye want? I have a blunderbuss, I warn ye."

"Is that you, Mr Balfour?" said Alan, stepping back and looking up. "I'll not tell ye my name, but there's something I think we ought to talk about."

"And what is it?" asked my uncle.

"David," said Alan.

"What was that?" cried my uncle, in a changed voice.

"Shall I shout the rest of the name, then?" said Alan.

"I'd better let ye in," said my uncle doubtfully.

"I don't know that I want to trust myself inside," said Alan, "You'd better come down here and talk to me."

It took Ebenezer a long time to get downstairs. At last, we heard the creak of the hinges. I saw Alan step back, while my uncle sat down on the top doorstep with the blunderbuss ready in his hands.

"If ye come a step nearer," I heard him say, "you're as good as dead. Now, let's hear what ye've got to say!"

"I am a Highland gentleman," Alan said. "My country is not far from the Isle of Mull where it seems there was a ship lost. The next day a gentleman of my family came upon a half-drowned lad. He took him to an old castle, where from that day to this he has been a great expense to my friends. When they found that he was your nephew, Mr Balfour, they asked me to look ye up. If you're not prepared to pay for the boy, you are not likely to see him again. My friends, ye see, are not well off."

"I don't care," my uncle said. "I'm glad to see the back of the lad. I'll pay no ransom for him."

"What!" said Alan. "You can't desert your brother's son!"

"I'll certainly say nothing about it," said my uncle drily.

"Then it'll be David that tells the story," said Alan.

"What's that?" my uncle cried.

"Well, if you won't pay for the lad, my friends aren't likely to keep him," answered Alan. "They'll let him go where he pleases."

"I don't care for that either," my uncle said.

"I was thinking that," said Alan.

"What do ye mean?"

"Why, Mr Balfour," replied Alan, "either ye like David and will pay to get him, or if ye don't want him, what do ye want done with him – and how much will ye pay?"

My uncle shifted uneasily on his seat.

"Come, sir," cried Alan, "I'm not standing here all night. Answer at once, or I'll ram my sword through you."

I heard my uncle scramble to his feet. "Eh, man," he cried. "Just tell me plain what ye want."

"Do ye want the lad killed or kept?" said Alan.

"We'll have no bloodshed," wailed my uncle.

"Ah," said Alan, "that'll cost more."

"Cost more?" my uncle gasped. "Would ye soil your hands with crime?"

"Hoots!" said Alan, "it's crime, either way. But it's easier to kill, and quicker and surer. It'd be a lot of trouble to keep the lad alive."

My uncle gave a kind of moan. "If I have to pay for it, I'll have to pay for it," he said.

"We'll have to agree upon the price," said Alan. "It's not very easy for me to say how much. I'd have to know what ye gave Hoseason, for instance."

"Hoseason!" squeaked my uncle. "What for?"

"For kidnapping David," said Alan.

"It's a lie!" my uncle cried.

"So you say," said Alan, "but ye shouldn't have trusted Hoseason."

"Did Hoseason tell ye?" cried Ebenezer.

"How else would I know," said Alan. "He and I are partners. The thing I don't know is how much you paid."

"Well," said my uncle, "He's a liar, and I gave him twenty pounds. But he was to have what he could get for selling the lad as a slave in America."

"Thank you, Mr Thomson. That will do very well,"

said the lawyer, stepping forward; and then, very politely, "Good evening, Mr Balfour," he added.

I stepped forward, too. "Good evening, Uncle," I said.

"It's a fine night, Mr Balfour," Torrance said.

My uncle stood like stone. Alan grabbed the blunderbuss from his hands. Then Mr Rankeillor plucked him from the doorstep and led him into the kitchen.

I think we were all filled with a sense of success, but I felt also a sort of pity.

"Come, come, Mr Ebenezer," said the lawyer, "don't be downhearted. Give us the cellar key, and Torrance shall draw us a bottle of your father's wine." Then, taking me by the hand, "Mr David," he said, "I wish you all joy in your good fortune, which I believe you deserve." And then to Alan, "Mr Thomson, you did very well."

We quickly had the fire lit and a bottle of wine uncorked. A good supper came out of Torrance's basket, to which Alan and I sat down. The lawyer and my uncle passed into the next room to talk together. At the end of an hour, my uncle and I signed the agreement which the lawyer had brought with him. By its terms, my uncle was to pay me two-thirds of the yearly income of Shaws.

When I lay down that night on the kitchen chests, I was a man of means and had a name in the country. Alan, Torrance and Rankeillor slept and snored on their hard beds; but I lay till dawn, looking at the firelight playing on the ceiling and making fine plans for the future.

CHAPTER SIXTEEN
Goodbye!

I still had Alan, who had helped me so much, on my hands. I felt, also, that something should be done to prove James of the Glens innocent of murder.

I talked of these things to Rankeillor the next morning, walking to and fro before the house of Shaws. The lawyer was quite certain that I must help Alan out of the country at whatever risk. He thought differently about the case of James.

"There is only one way you can give evidence in the matter and that's in a court of law," he said. "You might find yourself in the same pickle. You will say that you are innocent. Well, so is he. To be tried for your life before a Highland jury and with a Highland judge upon the bench might prove to be only a short step to the gallows."

"In that case, sir," I said, "I would just have to be hanged – would I not?"

"My dear boy," he answered, "you must do what you think is right. Go and do your duty, if you must – and be hanged, if you must, like a gentleman."

He wrote me two letters, one to his bankers, the British Linen Company, placing money in my name.

"You will need some at once to help your friend Mr Thomson," he said. "The only way you can help James of the Glens is to seek the advocate, tell him your tale, and offer your evidence."

The other letter was to a learned man of my own home, Mr Balfour of Pilrig.

"I think he will help you," said Mr Rankeillor "but I don't think you need say anything about Mr Thomson."

He shook hands with me and set out with Torrance for the Ferry, while Alan and I turned our faces to the city of Edinburgh. I looked back once at the house of my fathers. In one of the top windows, I caught a glimpse of my uncle staring after me, his head bobbing up and down and back and forward like the head of a rabbit from a burrow.

Alan and I spoke little as we walked. The same thought was in both our minds – that we were near the time of parting. We had arranged that Alan should go into hiding again at a place nearby, where I could reach him whenever I wanted. I was to find a lawyer who was an Appin Stewart and therefore to be trusted. He was to find a ship and make arrangements for Alan's voyage to France.

When we came within sight of the city, we knew that we had come to the parting of our ways. We went over the things that we had agreed between us – the address of the lawyer, the daily hour at which Alan might be

found, and the signals that were to be made by any who came seeking him. I gave him a few guineas that Mr Rankeillor had lent me so that he should not starve.

"Well, goodbye," said Alan, and held out his left hand.

"Goodbye," I said, and gave the hand a little grasp, and went off down the hill.

Neither of us looked the other in the face, nor so long as he was in my view did I take one look back at the friend I was leaving.

I passed into the streets of the city where the buildings, the crowds, the smell and the fine clothes struck me into a kind of daze so that I just drifted where my legs carried me. Yet all the time I was thinking of Alan and I was filled with a great sadness.

Luck was with me. My feet were guided in my drifting to the very doors of the British Linen Company's bank. I squared my shoulders and went inside, walking boldly and with pride. I was Mr David Balfour of Shaws.